So Dark, the Con of Man

JONATHAN K. WADE

CONTENTS

FOREWORD

It is perhaps necessary to prepare the reader for the rather heavy and bleak tone the story begins with for I introduce the main character at a rather pivotal moment in his life; a time of utmost emotional upheaval, as well as the convergence of his principle ideas, beliefs, and convictions that give rise to both his discontent and his eventual transcendent realisations. Needless to say, he was not always as troubled, angry, or hopeless as we find him to be at the onset. He was in fact quite a cheerful, adventurous, and optimistic young man. But through various provocative influences (books, people, travels, tragedies, loves, failures, etc.) during his life, he has reached a point where he feels he is drowning in mediocrity and crippled by the monotony of society.

The story is told through his tragic and despairing voice calling out from within the illusionary and seemingly colourful and prosperous Western middle class (the bourgeoisie – a rekindled term used throughout). This feeling is expressed by the character as he experiences the personal struggles with what he sees as the apathy and ignorance of the common man, and his deeply felt concern that Western culture is quickly losing touch with the high art and profound philosophical thinking that has brought it to such lofty heights. It is the awareness of our human predicament that casts our hero into the tumultuous period of spiritual chaos and turmoil as we meet him standing on the precipice of what he sees as humanity's next great overcoming, and the throes of what it is to bear such knowledge.

The character's mind has already plunged deeply into the heart of what poisons him, and although this may first appear cantankerous and melodramatic, there is a certain realism to his plight that cannot be denied, and this is revealed to the reader through his explosively spontaneous streams of thought. This story addresses the bleak, disenchanted, monotonous way of living that we house in Western materialism and conspicuous consumption, and that it is our spiritual happiness that goes unnourished and with that any sense of discovering our true self.

I request your patience to endure the romantic melancholy and passionate despair this novel initially presents. And despite its representation as a critique of modern society, it never lapses to the level of political tract. And so, it is perhaps better to consider this work as a poem; an outpouring of emotion, the point of which is to express the feelings of a tortured soul, one of us in some way or at some point, whose life has lost meaning and purpose, who has become fed up with the ongoing struggle of their life. In spite of this, there is, eventually, the revealing of meaning and a certain fulfilment, for above all else, this is a story of hope, but first, one must hear the hurt that echoes in the emptiness at the core of our modern existence.

To say this is a complete work of fiction would be untrue, for a great deal of that which takes place did indeed happen to our hero character in the real world; certainly a *roman à clef*. I mention this because, although the end product is 'fiction,' the reader will notice that the story is full of references to a select number of works that have directly influenced the character's understanding of himself and the reality and social context in which he exists. Of course, these references are woven into the story, but they are there, paraphrased, fragmented, expanded, or simplified, but always acknowledged and respected. They are there for the reason being, as I said, because much of that which the character is and holds dear and true, is the result of the exposure to the very real works or authors leading up to this point in time. To remove them entirely, and align this work with perhaps a truer sense of fiction, would be to remove the statements or ideas that had a profound, life-shattering effect on the character.

You may also find yourself, dear reader, asking why has the author written such a despaired, melancholic, and frustrated story; are we not already aware of the hardships that life has an awful tendency to deliver us or the great pangs of sadness drenching parts of the world in grief? Why not write something that is positively distracting or beautiful or hopeful? Why must you, the author, draw attention to the bitter realities of our everyday existence? Better that we forget ourselves and what we already know is painfully true. Well, to ignore the agony that may not affect you does not make it go away. To remain ignorant to bitter truths is a road to self-ruin and the continued hardship and poverty of society and humanity at large. As Nikolai Gogol said in his in-text justification for *Dead Souls*, 'The mind that might have come upon a sudden fountainhead of great resources [to aid the human psyche] is asleep.'[1] Without becoming properly inquisitive about what pains and depresses the human soul, we will continue to suffer to some degree; the better our ability to understand and place our anguish in context, the more apt we will be at reconciling it (to paraphrase de Botton's abstraction[2] of Marcel Proust). And that is what this story is; a view of the world that is as confronting as it is honest, and with the intention of bringing to light that very monotonous, daily suffering for the way our lives are ordered about in the hope of stirring within the reader that which is both human and loving; for that is all we are despite appearances.

PART I

ONE
A TEAR WELLED

A SOFT, EVENING BREEZE sings its way through the trees and ripples across the lake; the water shimmers as the setting sun casts flecks of gold across its surface. A frog stirs the sound of water; I return to chopping wood.[1] The handle is stained with sweat and blood, though my hands no longer bleed.

Sinking through the treetops the last dying rays of sun glint in my eyes as I glance upon a small wooden cabin huddling beneath the branches of two tremendous oak trees; its little windows glowing golden in the dwindling light. I let the axe gently fall from my hands, overcome by a slow moving wave of emotion filling my body. The breath is taken from me; a stunning turquoise and cobalt lake surrounded by a dense forest of lush conifers, oaks and maples, nestling within a deep valley of magnificent rocky mountains that tower all around; their snow-capped peaks vanishing into dark clouds as a deep purple and blue drape of twilight gently descends. I take a deep breath; the smell of the air rich with pine and wood and earth fill my senses. My fingertips tingling as a feeling of enchantment sweeps through me.

Where am I?

'Show me your face,' a voice whispers from the darkness.

I sat up, breathless and dizzy; the quilt a tangled mess. I looked down at my hands, searching for calluses, blood, or sweat but found nothing; a dream. I closed my eyes and took a deep breath, searching for those sweet odours of earth and tree and air that were so palpable only a moment ago. My body tingled, my legs restless and hot. I slumped back down onto my lumpy mattress and stared longingly at the cracked and flaky ceiling, filled with a glumness and frustration of having just been somewhere so delightful, so serene, and all of a sudden ejected back to this dreary reality of sleeplessness and despair.

I closed my eyes and beckoned sleep to return, but the slow, heavy footsteps of someone padded back and forth outside my apartment door. The old floorboards creaked with trepidation as whoever it was stalked repeatedly the length of the hallway. Soft and rhythmic the footsteps paced up and back; patient, marauding, hungry. I got up and treaded quietly out of the bedroom and forward to my apartment door. As I approached I could still hear the heavy footsteps trace the unwanted guest's path; the floorboards still groaning with nervousness. But as I put my ear to the door only nightly silence lingered. I waited a moment; my breath caught, but still, nothing. I unlatched the deadbolt quietly and waited but again nothing; no footsteps, no movement, no creaking floorboards. I turned the handle with a slow scraping of metal that echoed cringingly, opening the door slowly. The moonlight from the hallway crept into my apartment and across my bare feet. I stayed where I was but steadily pulled the door more and more open. My eyes were wide; my pupils dilated. My mouth was dry, and my throat barren. I waited; if the thing that had come had come to end me then its anticipation foreshadowed its own doing. Time had frozen and in that moment of nonsense I stepped across the threshold into the moonlight of the hallway. An open square stairwell worked its way up the centre of the building leaving a gaping shaft of cold emptiness from ground floor to top floor. I squinted across into the darkness at the decaying apartments, the crumbling bannister, but nothing seemed to disturb the stillness of the night.

The moon peeked through the skylight and shined on just my side of the open walkway, concealing the other three sides in darkness. My eyes were drawn to the ethereal line where moonlight met darkness with such distinction as a velvet curtain meets its stage. And beyond that veil, within that shadow, a pair of golden eyes did I meet. Its size and shape hidden from me, indistinguishable from the darkness that surrounded it, but those golden eyes, stirring like honey, were but a few feet from the ground.

It started to pant, hungry, eyeing its prey. I could hear its tongue smack its lips, whetting its teeth. Its eyes unflinching; stirring round and round. A tear welled as destiny spoke:

'Beware the beast that lurks in the dark, boy,' the wolf murmured, 'For your time has come.' It licked its lips once more before turning away, stalking off, its heavy footsteps lumbering, disappearing into blackness.

I felt a sudden coming-to and realised I was standing in my hallway at two in the morning. I turned and closed the door behind me, then I checked the peephole; nothing was there. *A dream within a dream.* I crawled back into bed, wondering if such a spot existed, a cabin by a lake. That would be a swell place I thought sleepily, before letting the veil return me to a forgotten slumber.

TWO
DEN OF THE BELLYACHERS

FLUORO LIGHTS BUZZED INCESSANTLY, sirens sounded, engines powered up and down, and re-rolling machines ran at full capacity. Forklifts screeched their rubber wheels and puffed plumes of black smoke into the air as they loaded and unloaded never-ending plastic rolls of well-strategized brand designs, capitalising on every possible unconscious glitch of psychological consumer inclination. Wrinkled faces hid alcoholism and hopelessness but winked and smiled when you caught eyes; defeated shift-workers digging their graves while dreaming of the lives they'll never have. And last but not least, the ever-present, barely audible shouts of floor managers bellyaching their unscrupulous *hear-ye's*. A fluorescent tomb of animated corpses, barely working and yet (depressingly) so far from living, donating their lives for... what? The serfs of Russia are not a forgotten people, look! There are some right here, in this unholy building of spirit crushing monotony; that is, an agreement signed in blood unavoidable to the rat that must turn the wheel and press the lever to get a crumb of cheese.

This is where I work; where the common man works, toils, watches his life evaporate if only he was not so disillusioned: the glory of opportunity, of a healthy economy, of being civilised, of being blessed and fortunate. The off-cuts of 'the dream' that didn't quite come to fruition so instead, an appeaseable settlement made, whereby instead of a life of jubilance and riches one contentedly accepts doing the utmost meaningless fussing about, and expresses gratitude that it is stable and offers overtime.

This is not the moaning of some resentful and lazy scoundrel but the voice of the drowning but not yet drowned. Stuck in between where I am and where I want to be, this labour I must endure; it is what we call 'making ends meet.' And it is here, in this lowly place (and places just like it) where so many a people are forced to carve out a certain gladness, a certain future from such little means, in our constant pursuit of happiness and deeper fulfilment that, tragically, receives such tiny attention and opportunity. And yet when we ask ourselves, 'what we feel like doing tomorrow, where we want to go next year, things we want to do with ourselves,' we feel so empowered, that such choices are every bit up to us, and of course, why wouldn't they be? And yet this is the very disillusion I just spoke of.

We are at the beck and call... It was just then that my train of thought was interrupted by the arrival of my bellyaching floor manager. I say unscrupulous because the demand for work is always more than what the worker can meet; this is how a company ensures dutiful employees, and how managers, often vicious dogs on leads in places such as this, become managers – by showing a willingness to give up their moral decency under the guise of being committed and loyal to the company. They'll bark at you, growl if you are slow or late or daydreaming, unperturbed by how hardworking you were yesterday or the day before or last week. They'll ask you to do more than you can, ask you to work overtime, ask you to work weekends, when you are sick, on your birthday or after your baby is born. When there are profits to be made there is often little reprieve. They have become unscrupulous because they have the company on their side but the company is not human and so has no humility; they are no longer one of you, a worker, a common man. Or so they think.

But this particular bellyacher never had the opportunity to tear at me, and he hated that. He was a late shift manager, and they were the worst of the lot. While the people from the office (the proper managers, and supervisors, and executives) moseyed on home hours ago, and were most likely cosily asleep in their warm beds with full bellies, the late shift was just kicking into gear, and with no one around to yank on their lead, these floor managers growled to their hearts content.

'Powe' down!' He snarled. 'It says 'ere (on his clipboard of never-endingness) yew got a meetin' tomorra'. Upstairs.'

White bubbles of saliva gathered at the corners of his thin, cracked lips when he spoke. But the bellyacher doesn't look at me, he just taps his pen on his clipboard with his cigarette stained fingers. *Tap tap tap.*

'With who?'

'What?' He snapped.

'Who is the meeting with? What for?' We have to

yell at each other to be heard above the machines.

'Oh. Some woman in a suit. HR.' *Tap tap tap.* 'Farked if I know – maybe they realised yew ain't such a hotshot after all.'

Now he looks at me, producing a condescending smile of decaying teeth full of gaps under a bulbous nose; a grin that stretches across his poorly shaven chin of white and grey stubble. His pockmarked face possesses an unusual stupidity and yet he makes double what I do. This was his custom, to make unsettling jibes as a show of his authority and not realising his bitter resentment came from being just another brick in the wall.

'Well, get back to work yew shit.'

This was my day; ten hours of absurd monotonous labour, harassed occasionally by the unscrupulous bellyachers, and all for what? The truth of my current situation – not that I (or anyone) am fully aware of when one aspect of their life comes to an end and a new one begins – was that this really was just one of life's interludes. They are all interludes, and the absurdity of this employment will surely be replaced over and again. That is of course until I find the illusive resolution my soul seeks.

It takes me close to an hour by train to get home,

but most nights I get off a couple stops early and walk the quiet, empty streets. This adds another half hour to my night but it is the sweetest half hour of my discontented days.

THREE
LOST FOR WORDS

THE NIGHT WAS NO DIFFERENT TO ANY OTHER; dark and still, cold and empty. My breath steaming, catching in the foggy glow of the odd streetlamp. The sounds of train horns linger in the crisp air and the crunching echo of my footsteps on the wet asphalt makes me feel strangely as though I'm not so alone. I watch the distant traffic lights for the next mile flick through their green-yellow-red cycles over and over without a single car passing through. Up ahead the *H-Mart* on the corner radiates its salvation-like white glow; a way station for ungodly-hour shift-workers, narcoleps and druggies. A place of rescue where one finds not bread and wine but plastic-wrapped food of an enduring shelf-life and cigarettes; the communion for a *twenty-four-seven* society. But I don't go in; nothing in there for me. It's the walk I cherish; the quiet, the open air, the empty streets. When the world sleeps it's interesting what the woken mind stumbles onto or into. What doors it unlocks, what rabbit-holes it falls down.

It's during these walks that I couldn't help but feel entirely outside the world of convention, of conversation, of endless to-ing and fro-ing. Pained all too often by my half-hearted attempts to play along in the little charade we affectionately call life. Guilty of my half-truths, shamed by my two-facedness, accountable, perhaps more than most, for an honest reaction to it all. An honest interpretation rightfully mine, which most unrightfully wish not to hear.

Every night I think of how the mill turns, the rats' race, how oblivious to the ineptitude to which he – the common man – renders himself; quietly yielding to a reality far from unfolded yet relishing miserably in the mediocrity of his self-imposed futility. You have tried to do everything you were taught, tried to fit into the world by becoming the thing you are not, and within this failure, within this dissonance you still crave the fruits of happiness, it has become conscious in you, but still you continue to consume the carrion of your past's deception despite how unnourishing it is. Addicted to your false idols, nauseated by your inadequacy, and yet too ignorant to hold yourself responsible, too blind, too pathetic, too weak to turn the tide yearning to be turned. So instead you flounder, always in pursuit and never in obtainment. You are every bit greedy; still tempted by entitlement and status and ego. Never stopping to realise that what you need is what you are, and what you are is everything you need. And all this in a time of abundance and revelry, and perhaps why I feel so tired, so bored; exhausted by the endless monotony of our age despite the dizzying heights of the intellectual man. A vista wasted on the thoughtless and bended knee. Floating on the surface of what others find meaningful and joyous. Panged by their ignorance; stifled is the music that reaches my ears, drowned out by the incessant chatter of a world so successful at being suppressed, so successful at suffocating itself.

And yet I can't help but feel removed from the run of the common man. I find myself more and more looking down at the ordinary life and feeling proud that I somehow escaped it, that I have not been poisoned by it. And yet, in spite of all my frustrations and grievances, here I am, wandering these streets, this concrete steppe, dreary from labour, delirious from spite. *Where are all the trees?* There is little for me here, but so I feel little anywhere else. It is a curse 'the greener grass,' a dream for dreamers. No, what we have is always before us, not at horizon's end but at arm's reach, only we do not like what has been put there, only we are too weak to hand it back and say, 'this is no good to me, this is no good for most of us.'

And so I walk the streets, between the drudgery of my labour and the sweetness of sleep, guided by a billion stars shimmering and shining, plumbing eternal questions of which no answer will do, which no answer there is, and wonder hopelessly why – *why any of it?* Their company more breathtaking than anything this trivial world of men has offered me.

I noticed a wall of fresh graffiti; 'the stars shine brightest in the darkest of night.' *Oh, and how true*, for all my nights have once again become dark.

There is no helping the fact that I feel alone in this menial world of things. Not hopelessly alone for I support some relations; one or two dear friends, a lover (*if only I were capable of true love*), and a string of acquaintances better known as friends, if only we all weren't so caught up in the clumsy web of regard.

My dear Hesse, your words echo in the halls of time, and still faintly, I hear them: 'our struggle to find the trail of the divine in the midst of this life we lead, in this besotted humdrum age of spiritual blindness.'[1] How true you were then, but how can it still yet be true today? *One hundred years on* and still we fear living and loving. I too cannot for long linger in those places with the suffocating and obtrusive music. The only books I can read are decades old, the news of today and its triteness is finally lost on me despite the daily horrors that the poor folk must endure. The hoards that fill the cities, the traffic, the packed trains and shopping malls filled with insatiable consumers. Its architecture, its business, its politics – behold the *civilised* man in all his horrendous splendour. I cannot understand what drives people to imbed themselves in phony lives. I cannot understand the lust for bars and cafes, the lust for clothes and gadgets, the yearning to be noticed or regarded for such shallow value. I cannot understand the personal and spiritual sacrifice to forgo living to be a slave of simple gratifying comforts. And yet all of these things are in my grasp, for which thousands of others around me strive, and yet I cannot bring myself to swallow their obvious false sentiment; these joys I cannot understand nor stomach; and so this life I struggle to bear.[2]

It is true, or at least clear, that I am grieving, grieving for the present day, for all the countless hours and days that brought me nothing significant, nothing pleasurable, that were lost in mere passivity and dullness, that I spent mindlessly marching to the beat of some oppressor's drum. *Yes, that was it.* This is my sorrow, lead astray to find neither home nor joy nor nourishment in a world that is strange and incomprehensible to me. A world handed down to me of which I cannot return and can only lament.

I hope not to be mistaken; I am not who am I because of some unlucky turn of events. I have not been rejected by parent or society. I am not poor (or rich) or uneducated. I am every part average and ordinary, and these the fetters of my plight. I have failed to tear loose that part of my soul that was breastfed on conventions and comforts, on the whiskey'd nip to pacify the bourgeois despite having long since differentiated myself from the prosaic substance of its shoddy ideals and beliefs.

I longed for days past; of simpler times of simpler living. To hitchhike with drifters and beatniks; to own one shirt, one coat, and one pair of jeans; and to wear them till I wore holes in them and then some. To see towns I had never heard of, would never see again, and yet never forget; because the country was so vast and so untraveled, and took you weeks and months to get from one end to the other, and in the back of flatbeds was how it was done: painfully slow and full of honest adventure and beauty.

How I wished to know how to bail hay or fix a barn or plough a field. To be an oilman or rancher or drover. And to do these things for a summer rather than a lifetime, and just because and nothing more than for some food and gas money. To hitch my way from coast to coast, to lose myself in the heat of a jazz bar, to write postcards and be bailed out with a wire transfer. To *live* damn it. But no, I existed now; soft and insular, self-conscious and prideful. The world viewable from our bedroom, the recognition of rock bands but not plant life, more attracted to ridiculous celebrities and their spoutings than we are to scientific achievements, valuing athletic ability more than artistic vision; hack music assembled by hack artists flood the airwaves and drown the youth. We drink average coffee in intentionally understated parlours making them paradoxically fancy and me by association, all the while pretending that this all has some innate value, that this is somehow what purposeful or sincere living surmounts to today; this frenetic inauthenticity. What a ghastly realisation if only it were realised, and all this under the nose of our progressive, modern world.

And what confounds one further is that each generation is capable of knowing so much more than the one previous, so much more aware of social unrest, injustice, or human tragedy in the far reaches of the globe (certainly not here, in the warm bosom of the bourgeois home), and yet we make that that awareness alone somehow makes us more moral, more upstanding. Perhaps this is why we do so little about it, as though the awareness alone is enough, and that it is someone else's problem to fix because it's all just a bit hard for me to help, I already have such little time to spare, or maybe I don't want to do anything about it because it doesn't really affect me. I'll just turn my head or change the channel, and then drown it all in bitter coffee and hack music and hack art, in purposeless purpose to avoid the moral obligation of actually behaving better... because that would mean sacrifice. And the bourgeois' world is rich and abundant and truly unsacrificing and selfish. So instead we delude ourselves with a brief prayer or discussion on the travesties of some foreign and faraway place wrecked by civil war or poverty or slavery, and deem that enough consideration for our part, and go right on back to milling.

Perhaps I'm romanticising about days gone by when we knew less and the world wasn't so small and so our dreams were bigger, but I don't mind. Better than the unromantic banality of today, which, to the glorified simpleton is brimming with glory. The world of today is manufactured, artificial, and above all else calculated. Measured for profit, measured for consumption but poorly measured for waste and destruction and self-ruin. That is the truth of it if you dare to hear it.

The self-absorbed hobby rules the common man; obsessed and addicted he dedicates so much energy towards something that has such microscopic value. And not just hobbies but all manner of life really; the jock, the conservative, the old-timer, the God-fearing, the fashionista, the narcissist, the corporate slave, the sexualised self-objectified, even the modern day hipster – the outspoken rebel to the beast that is capitalism – expresses himself out of trendiness rather than honest poverty or rebellion. The truth is there is no poverty in the bourgeois city, only poverty of soul and spirit to earnestly experience something authentic, something gripping; instead we play at life like a merry-go-round visiting the same places feeling the same things waving like blubbering children as the pretty pictures wiz by. Sure it looks like we're moving but we're not, we're just going round and round and priding ourselves on how much we see, 'oh look at that, oh look at this.' Round and round.

I stopped in front of an old, vacated building with boarded-up windows; the grimy bricks looked black, but whether from paint or pollution I couldn't tell. The building appeared to have once been a ticket office for theatre shows: old posters were pasted on top of one another three or four deep; holes, tears, and rain damage revealed what came and went, but none were new. No one around here cares because no one goes.

I continued on into the quiet cold, the street lit up and flashing like cheap Christmas lights, wondering when was the last time he went to the theatre, the opera, the symphony, the ballet, the art galleries? When was the last time he discussed poetry or paintings or philosophy? What man knows Nietzsche, the immortal?[3] All this, once the height of cultured revelry, how they have evaporated from the senses of common man.

Our docility towards the arts reflects a docility of our want for deeply layered and provoking stimulation. We've been tempted, caught, and now dulled. We have been lead to believe there is a formula for happiness and a fulfilled life, but if there is then show me the cities or nations where everyone is happy and fulfilled. Well, there aren't any. Perhaps show me the cities and nations that at least have a formula (or a pill) to 'cure' depression and anxiety (the opposite of happiness and fulfilment) – oh, well, they are everywhere. Well then, it seems we have established our playing field. The powers that be understand very well how to make you work and slave and consume, and the powers that be understand very well how to fix you up so you can continue to work and to slave and to consume. But it appears the powers that be have very little to do with guiding us to happiness and fulfilment. One might even suggest that the very first step would be to do the very opposite of working, slaving, and consuming, because the current run of the mill, the merry-go-round of our insular, boring, and predictable lives is drowning us in our own watery reflections.

Everybody is doing what they think they're supposed to be doing and they try so hard to prove it.

Only, no one really knows what they're supposed to be doing – work hard, buy a house, and get married. And we can scarcely do that with much success today. It's a sad state of affairs, and yet, as detached as I may have become, I am nonetheless still here, shackled to this time and place and all too often think myself to a depressed stupor.

And yet, as prepared for it all as we try to be, there is no avoiding life's blunders (for I am surely blundering now), and one must remember that they often reveal an unsuspected world whereby we find ourselves at the mercy of forces that are not rightly understood. Suppressed desires and conflicts are the very energies that bring forth these blunders often in the form of hidden doors, rabbit-holes, and heralds in our dark dreams. What they are not is the merest of chance; they are the unsuspected springs rippling on the surface of life.[4]

'I smell you, boy.' A grumbling voice drifted in the darkness.

I stopped, peering sideways into the shadows of the narrow alleyway that ran between two tall buildings. *Yes, this is why I wander the steppes.* All of a sudden I felt alive, filled with a sense of throbbing curiosity where others would likely be filled with fear. And fearing what – a knife in the belly for my wallet, or perhaps death? Why fear death, something so honest and true. Something, perhaps the only thing, which we shall all experience together in its absolute. No, this was not a thief or a murderer, not a beggar or a drifter. This, for the moment, was just a voice.

'And what is it you smell?' I replied.

After a long and contemplating silence, 'Hunger,' the voice said. 'The hunger in you is strong. The hate, the fury. The world of sheep ignites you.' The voice laughed long and slow, rasping till it faded.

I turned and faced the alleyway and saw nothing but darkness. *Not even moonlight shines here.* Silently, the cold air steamed with each of my fast, anxious breaths; I took a step forward and the voice rasped with pleasure. A pair of yellow eyes watched me unblinkingly from the shadows; they rose slowly from the ground, the voice taking shape. He stayed in the dark, but I could sense him; old and beaten, but a beast still.

'Show me your face,' the voice grumbled.

'What?'

'Tell me,' he licked his lips, 'why do you prowl the streets, boy?'

'Well, they say the eyes of an owl are dimmed by the midday sun, and maybe so too are our wits.'

The eyes laughed hard, choking him with lust and spite. Then silence once more. His yellow eyes levelled on me, holding me. I could have run, but something of him would chase me, catch me and bite down on me. And it would scar my soul, filling it with a poison, a regret that I didn't stay and risk myself.

'Are you a parrot, boy? A preened parrot inside a gilded cage?'

'No.'

'Again,' the voice grumbled, '*why do you prowl the streets?*' His eyes narrowed, the yellow turned to amber, stirring round and round like honey in a pot.

I waited a moment. 'There is calm behind the silence. There is calm in me.' I said thoughtfully. 'My thoughts are long and lucid; my mind wanders, plumbing the depths of our human predicament. I am filled with a curiosity that is deafened during the day. I go places I haven't been before. I feel excited.'

'You feel *powerful.*'

'Y-yes.'

'Why?'

'Because... I am awake and they are asleep. But in

their sleep they are vulnerable and truthful. More so than they are during the day.'

'And you?'

'I... I am aroused by the vastness of the night. I feel alive. We are all trapped, walled inside these cities, but at night, at night I remember what it feels like to escape, to explore –'

'– to hunt,' the voice growled.

To hunt?

'I fear your puzzle is still in pieces boy, but from one dying wolf to another, I shall give you a key,' the voice said from the shadows, the molten amber eyes unblinking.

'Man can only live intensely at the cost of himself,' the voice, the eyes, the *shadow* began, 'but the common man treasures nothing more highly *than* himself, as basic and little as he has become. And so he opts for preservation and security at the cost of intensity and passion. A fool's trade. He has extinguished his own inner fire, his fervour for living, preferring to harvest a quiet and obedient mind over a cunning and inquisitive intellect. He has chosen cheap comforts for pleasure, convenience for independence, substituted majority for power, order for force, and the ballot box for responsibility. All proof that the common man is a weak creature, fearful, anxious, and above all else, far too willing to give himself away.[5]

'And because of his weak and petty character, the common man does, and always will play the role of a herd of sheep among free roving wolves. In whatever numbers he exists in, he is useless in driving man forward or higher, for left to his own devices he will progress at nothing. Worse than that, he cannot even maintain himself. And while he chooses to live in such a way there is nothing that will avail to save him; no organisation or institution, nor common sense, nor virtue. And yet the common man prospers – why? Because of the rare and lonely wolves in his midst.'[6] He rasped with great pleasure once again; the sound echoing up between the two buildings, fading as it climbed.

'The success of society has not been made so by the successes of the common man. It is only by virtue of the all-encompassing and pervasive nature of the society that surrounds him that he is able to benefit, and be pulled up and forward by those who are of unique mind and vision, and who cast themselves off in the pursuit of new knowledge, and ultimately, whose stunning revelations and sparks of insight are embraced and absorbed by the common man as his own. The life energy of the bourgeoisie by no means courses through the veins of the common man, but in those of the lonely wolves, the outcasts and thinkers, the immortals.[7] It is his thirst and hunger that drives him to break free of his cage, to roam, to stray, to risk a cold and lonely existence for a single night of thrilling discovery. But despite his solitude, his self-reliance and self-rule, despite his evolution beyond the common man, he is nevertheless bound by his borders, a captive whose intellectual triumphs and personal glories will eventually be scavenged upon. The greatest trickery played on the common man is making him believe that he is a sheep in a sheep's skin, and not realising that the transformation to wolf is always within him. And so, there are many thousands of lives and minds all on the precipice of great transformation, who would have already acknowledged their inner fire, their hunger for truth, had they not been so pacified by the gruel of their spoon-fed opportunities, and so fastened to the mill by childhood sentiments. Instead, they take their neighbourhood for their country, their nation for the world, and their patriotism for reason;[8] and so, they linger, obey, and oblige themselves with their fellow man, lacking the courage or the knowhow to shed their false skin, and rejoice in the moonlight of their divine free will.'

The voice fell silent as two men, fresh from communion, walked past the alleyway; their conversation pausing as they met me with a queer glance. I nodded a kind of arbitrary gesture, hoping to avoid suspicion or inquiry from them. The tall one squinted, dragging on his cigarette, the amber end glowing hotly; the short fat one hocked and spat, then they walked on.

The beast's liquid golden eyes began to dim as he continued, 'In time, most wolves of the steppe will compromise, resigning themselves to the sad ideals of the bourgeoisie. Eventually, they return to the hollow throng, adding to its strength, and hopelessly sharing with it the glory of their wolfish nights. This is their last resort, to forsake themselves in order to live. A bitter and miserable end to a once courageous and willing soul. There are but a few who burst through to the heavens every so often; their destiny is beyond bondage, their gifts universal. The souls of this order are rewarded in a world beyond this one; departing in splendour their deliverance unconditional. They wear the thorn crown and their number is small,'[9] the voice grumbled distantly.

The eyes shifted in the shadows before starting up

again, 'We often meet our destiny on the roads we dare not take. For all this to be true, a lonely wolf must plumb the depths of his chaotic inner soul and dare to take the leap into the unknown. He that loseth his soul shall find it,'[10] he cackled. 'Piece by piece the riddle of his existence is revealed to him each time he plunges into the murky waters of his unconscious, the ocean for which all the universe swims. And each time a pearl is found, a treasure of truth discovered and brought forth in its absolute and changeless form.'

'I fear I have entered such murky waters before and yet have returned empty handed.'

He rasped loudly, his honeyed eyes stirring once again. 'It is not *one* such journey, or few, but many you must endure. Did you think returning from the other side, from beyond the veil was so easy, boy? That bringing back pearls of infinite wisdom or visions of ineffable truth was as easy as slipping in and out of bed?' His voice was like gravel.

A long silence followed. Our breath fogging in front of us; the beast in the shadows, his eyes glowing amber still.

'Slowly,' the voice began again, 'after each journey from the unknown you will be less and less able to re-join the throng of thoughtlessness, choosing instead to nuzzle the bosom of your own bourgeoning ways. But how long will it feed you, nourish you? How long will you survive on your own wandering the steppes? This still remains a hellish world of men, and will do so for many moons to come. And one-day man and wolf will be compelled to look each other in the eye without the mask of the other. One soul will survive, it will break through to the cosmic plateaus of the starry night and rejoice with all the other immortals that chose to ascend to loftier heights; the other will be devoured, not by beast but by man and his banality.[11] Fate brings on a thousand possibilities that await you between now and then; for the atmosphere of magical possibilities surrounds those willing to tread a single step outside the mill of common man.'

'And what of you? I see no thorned crown, only the shadow of a beast who lurks in the dark.' I said boldly and regretted it.

The beast reached out, thrusting an arm from the darkness; it was covered in coarse black hair, his skin weather-beaten, creased and cracked like old leather. *A man's arm.* A wrinkled and faded tattoo of a large serpent coiled around an anchor covered the inside of his forearm. He was clutching a little black book; its spine barcly holding, its edges ragged

'A key,' he grumbled, amber eyes staring, 'a key to unlock the door even *you* fear to enter. For the common man to live as he does he must be blind to the infinite... but this is not you,' he rasped.

I went to take it from him but his hand held it tight, 'You walk a path filled with danger and peril. You will forfeit many things lovely and pretty and sweet in this world, but to be the boon-bringer takes great sacrifice and it is a harsh destiny not always fulfilled.'

His gnarled hand let go and receded into the darkness. His amber eyes dimmed to a soft yellow and then disappeared altogether. I took a step towards the shadowed wall of the alley where the voice spoke from but found nothing but a cold and dark emptiness. I sensed the man, the voice, was no longer there; the beast had drifted back into the night, the cosmic.

I stepped back into the street and under the soft buzz of a streetlamp I held the book up:

THE TREATISE ON THE LOST SOULS:
A BOOK FOR EVERYONE AND NO ONE

FOUR
IN HER HEART OF HEARTS

MY WALK HOME WAS DREAMLIKE AND FOGGY; spellbound by the voice in the alley. *That beast in the dark.* Blocks passed without my knowing; my mind was a blur, a torrent of consciousness erupting, folding in on itself, crashing over and over. Nothing was coherent; I was cold, dizzy, and my heart raced. When I finally reached my apartment I had a throbbing headache. There was no question if any of it was real, if the apparition did indeed lurk forth from the cosmic for in my hand I clutched the little tattered book; and so eager was I to turn its yellowed pages.

I lived in a two-bedroom apartment on the top floor of a very old nineteenth-century building; it was cold in the winter and hot in the summer, the floorboards creaked and everywhere the paint was peeling. The wiring was decades old and the lights buzzed until they got warm. And there was no elevator, which is why I lived on the top floor. The landlady was an old Jewish woman, Ms Lieberman, whose father owned the building; he and his wife were dressmakers in the fifties but she died in childbirth and he followed a few years later from drinking too much. Alone and unmarried, Ms Lieberman became a recluse, shutting herself off from the world around her. She sold the dressmaking business, never married, and became a widow, 'the widow that never married,' they called her. Or so it goes.

Strangely, I was reminded of the sadness of the story almost every time I entered the building; not because I felt it to be particularly tragic but because of something else entirely. The only reason I could afford such a spacious apartment on the top floor is because it was formerly Ms Lieberman's; that was until a year or so after my moving in she fell and broke her hip. Prior to this she had grown quite fond of me; I had formed a habit of sitting with her and drinking tea once a week or so. She was a lovely lady with large, grey, bulging eyes, a blunt nose, rosy-red cheeks and a double chin. Her kind face positively breathed warmth and welcome. She seldom had guests but always seemed busy; in the winter she'd sit by the furnace and knit, in summer she'd walk to the park and feed the ducks. Quiet if not shy, and yet in times of misfortune or anguish she always offered sound advice or comforting words.

And yet despite this solitude she had kept her wits and talked to me often about the lives of young people today, curious about the changing of times as the world sped her by. When she hurt herself she was no longer able to climb the stairs and so acquired an apartment on the bottom floor while generously allowing me to take hers at no extra cost. Soon after her relocation she placed a tall mahogany cupboard in the foyer, and on either side of her door she had placed two plants in large pots on low stands; one was an azalea of lovely pink flowers, and the other an araucaria.

What reminded me of the lonely, sad, and perhaps forgotten Ms Lieberman every time I walked past was this: the fragrance of floor polish and turpentine mixing in with the rich mahogany; her always swept front step; the washed leaves of the plants and their scent, and how they were always well-watered. I was reminded of how much time she must have, how much time she has had all these years to tend to life's little habits and tasks, and how superfluous they were. And it was this that always made me think of the common man and his superfluity; he may not have a mahogany cupboard to lacquer or an azalea to wipe and water, but he certainly has given himself trifling little habits all the same.

Most evenings I would return to a vacant apartment; my daily life summarised by the stacks of books, manuscripts, and essays that piled the spaces and neglect for ordinary life. I didn't read because I thought myself an intellect or superior in some way, no, I read because I always thought myself thoroughly ordinary, and I hated that. And so to escape the repetitive daily humdrum of thoughtlessness that I knew I was prone to, I read as many of the greats as I could; thinkers beyond my comprehension, and I would re-read them until I at least vaguely understood them. And in them I knew I would find a tremor previously unheard, a vibration of life that strummed pure and beautiful, that hummed for just my ears. And despite my fatigue, and despite the hammer beating inside my skull, I could not wait to peer into this little book that I knew was mad; for all things great are at first a little crazy.

But not tonight.

As I stood at my door, the delicate scent of a sweet perfume lingered, a scent that once ignited a burning lust deep inside me. *And now?* She lay on the sofa, sleeping; her face turned angelic by the glow of a silent television blearing its nothingness. She was a beautiful thing, young and sweet with brown hair and brown eyes. She had come floating into my world on a summer's breeze – and don't all the love stories ring like that? During our first months together she would stay up all night and listen to me ramble, enchanted by my intellectual novelty like a doe-eyed little girl listening to her grandfather tell tender stories of faraway places. I spoke deliriously, captivated by her adoration, her round eyes, her pale skin, and her nakedness. Ideas and philosophies unravelled with poetic liveliness; I had never shared such fervour with anyone before. She found me deep and mysterious, and we made passionate, youthful love to each other; it was all very romantic, I suppose. But for the sensible person you cannot hang your hat on such mysteries and excitements, and she was in the end, very sensible.

She knew what she wanted to do with herself but didn't know what she wanted to get out of life; I wanted to wring it out of her. The passion was there for us, but over time the realities had begun to form cracks. And as I had done before in my dejected life, bit-by-bit I was withdrawing more and more, not just from her but from the call to fulfil my wretched social destiny as well. Not intentionally, not coldly, but painfully all the same.

She knows I'm different, but how different I guess I don't even know. She's young, heartfelt and foolish, and so still finds me deep and intriguing; my passions and convictions are mysteries to her, not a warning. But the more I question the state of the world and humanity's place in it, the less it all seems to make sense, the less I want to be a part of it. I was retreating once again into the darkness of my hermitage, except this time I had a sweet little trinket from the surface that wanted to laugh and dance and make babies one day. More recently, this realisation made me feel guilty and ashamed.

We were still in a good place for the most part – whatever that meant (she said it often). But it was nights like tonight that would start a fight; I would come home later than normal because of my star-lit wanderings, and this would upset her. She would first question why I'd go off instead of coming straight home; it wasn't jealousy, she was too practical for that. But she was afraid that she wasn't wanted for, afraid for why I didn't need to rush home to spend every waking moment with her, afraid for her future. And this reoccurring theme in her discontentment was always expressed by her concern for my lack of career (which meant money, which meant stability, which meant she could keep on loving me). She would say things like, 'But you are educated, and smart, *any* company would want you.'

And I would respond with painful ideological negativity; 'Yes, but I'm not sure *I* want any company. I mean is this it? Is this the point in my life where I say, 'this place is as good as any to start my career?' Why this company and not some other? Why this industry, this position, this city even? Aside from the world seeming almost infinite in its occupational variety, do people just forget that they happened to do all but one or two things they perchance stumbled into, and then *that* somehow becomes their professional legacy? 'Oh, I had so much choice and time, I could have been anything I wanted, but in the end I chose to be a seller of insurance, or a personal assistant of endless paper-shuffling to the executive so-and-so, or a number cruncher of endless bookkeeping, or a travelling salesman?'' And I would always answer her very serious questions with such roundabout responses. She hated that, and I always felt bad afterward.

What she really wanted was reassurance, of course. To know that this was something real and lasting and blossoming like a relationship should; with romance and vacations and a house and friends and marriage and laughter. Guarantees, as they were, proofs that she was getting what she was supposed to out of her neatly organised and preordained life: a good husband with a good job, and one or two but certainly not three little bundles of joy in the not too distant future. I used to feel bad for not being able to deliver such material fixtures, but long ago I realised the guilt came from the bourgeoisie and the coercion of its unenvious ideals.

And despite being every bit honest, and more honest by far than most, this was not what she wanted. And it is becoming clear that she will never understand me because I like too many different things, I question too many 'matter of facts' of life, and often get myself hung up and confused running from one falling star to another. *Ah, this is the night, and what it does to you.* And truth be told I had nothing to offer anyone except my own delirious confusions. A fact I would laugh sadly at when on my own.

She was only a couple of years into her career, and a shining example of how well the bourgeoisie nurture their little lambs so that they are loyal and optimistic, faithful and predictable. How ironic that this is precisely their Achilles heel; to not recognise but even worship that which rules and ruins them. The Stockholm syndrome of their hopes and dreams. Only I am not her captor, and she will one day have the choice to leave it for what it is thinking it what it isn't.

And like all the other nights that were made upset by this fruitless questioning to which I had no answers, she would ask me to hold her tight, tell me to say that I loved her, and go to sleep hoping deep within her little heart of hearts that it will all go as it should.

FIVE
THAT'LL BE ALL, BILL

THE NEXT EVENING, I was well into my shift by the time my floor manager, the gapped-tooth bellyacher, informed me 'they' were waiting for me upstairs. It was like crossing worlds as I went from the factory floor, through the glass doors, and into the main office; a place I only saw once – when I was taken on a walk-through during my first interview. A completely gratuitous showing of the prestige and reputation I would have the honour of working for and upholding should I get the job.

There were administrators, personal assistants, sales teams, team leaders, executives, and even directors all fussing around while maintaining an affluent air of sociability. There were lush green plants in pots, free-to-use coffee machines, framed pictures on the wall – a tropical island, Mt Everest, a Parisian cityscape (I wondered how many of these people would ever see these places), a noticeably pleasant ambient room temperature, and even laughter. I wasn't fooled though; I could smell him or her, the one who detested their job, that secretly wished embarrassment or emotional suffering on one of their co-workers. That fantasised about how glorious their last day would be smiting colourfully those that caused them so much mental anguish for so many years.

And then came the looks as I walked through covered in sweat and grease and ink spray. A blue-collared worker producing the very things they need to survive and yet judged with downcast eyes for doing just that. The flippant nature of the common man is soaked in hypocritical regard; 'we are both slaves you fools,' I wanted to say but such an obvious sentiment would be lost if they had already realised it.

I walked into the office and my floor manager's manager was in the room, Mr Thompson; the person that hired me, and who I hadn't seen since I was hired.

'This is Ms Anderson,' he said without acknowledgment, 'from HR.'

'Please, call me Sally.' She said warmly, inviting me to take a seat.

His phone began to ring, 'I'm sorry, Sally,' he said checking the caller, 'I'm going to have to take this.'

'Of course,' she said smiling. She was an attractive woman, very pleasing to look at despite perhaps being middle-aged. She wore her blonde hair pulled tight in a bun that showed off her delicate face; round blue eyes and full pink lips, a little nose and a slight dimple on her chin. She accentuated this with her posture, her perfume, a tight grey pencil skirt and white silk blouse cut high under her neck, and a calm if not overly-poised demeanour.

'So, as you know I'm from *Human Resources*,' her voice soft and kind, 'and the company wants to make some changes to improve quality and performance, amongst other things.'

'So, why am I here? I'm a good worker.'

'Well, that's just it,' She paused to smile, 'You're *very* good.' She opened up a file in front of her.

She looked over the pages and continued, 'You are one of the most efficient workers this company's ever had. You've never missed your quota, you have the least wastage, the lowest error rate, the highest accuracy for turnover, you've hit *all* targets, never been late, never taken a sick day, and I'm told you're the only *roller* to assist on a press. All that and you've only been here six months. Why?' She said interestedly.

'I-I don't know?' It seemed strange to justify why you did your job well.

'Why do you work so hard, Will?'

'I don't know. I'm here, although there's no point to what I'm doing, there seems less of a point to do it badly.'

She was taken aback by that. 'Really? There's no point to what you do?'

'Not really,' I said frankly. 'It requires no acumen, little skill, and in five or ten years machines will be doing factory labour anyway.'

'*Hmm,*' She looked confused. 'Are you bored, Will?'

'Of course.'

'Oh. Do you think you could do more, handle more responsibility?'

'Well, yeah, but so could most of the people here.'

'H-how do you mean?'

'Anyone can do what I do, and no offence but with the right opportunities most people could do what you do. I'm not saying what you do is easy, at all, but I am saying it isn't hard.'

Slightly stunned, 'Would you care to elaborate?'

'Well, every person is born capable, more than capable. What makes them *incapable* is the hand they were dealt – their social class, their ethnic background, what kind of school they went to, the teachers they had, whether or not their parents worked one job or three. The stories we're told and told to believe.'

'The stories?'

'The stereotypes, the labels, the belief structures about what's achievable for 'someone like you'. Television, the media, Sunday school; they're all just peddling a story, a reality for you to buy into, that you can relate to, follow, and one day become. If you come from a good home in a good neighbourhood you should go to a good school and get a good job: a lawyer, a doctor, a HR consultant. If you come from a broken home in a bad area you'll probably go to a bad school and well, a life in the service industry or hard labour awaits. Either or it has little to do with whether or not at some point you *were* capable.'

'So, what you're saying is the education and social systems are failing people, not the people themselves?'

'Well yes and no, but that's not my point. My point is life really comes down to two things; attitude and opportunity. The truth is, you can have everything and become nothing, and you can have nothing and become everything. Sure the system is corrupt but it's passive, it's not alive, it's not out to get you. It may look that way but that's an attitude. For sure it will chew you up and spit you out, but only if you let it. The system is what it is and it won't change overnight. What matters is how you respond to it; do you become something and make the system work for you, or do you become nothing and work for the system?'

'Okay. And how does this relate to *anyone* doing what I do?'

'Somebody once said, everybody is a genius, but if you judge a fish by its ability to climb a tree, it will live its whole life believing that it's stupid.[1] The tragedy of this modern age is that people allow themselves to be painted into a corner, put in a box, and by the time they finish school and reach a level of thinking that affords them some kind of perspective on things, *if* they manage to develop some kind of perspective on things, it's often too late and too hard to do anything about it.'

She sat with her arms crossed.

'So,' I continued, 'could half the guys in B building do what you do? Yes. But more importantly, were they given the opportunity or instilled with the right attitude to become it? Not a chance. Which is why they're down there and you're up here.'

'Is that so?' She was frowning. 'And yet here *you are*, full of perspective and attitude, or so it seems. Why are you working for the system, Will? Why are *you* down there?'

'You know, I ask myself the exact same question,' I said sarcastically.

'Maybe you think it's too late, too hard to change, and you're frustrated because you're wasting your time but there's nothing you can do about it.'

Unlike the many that happily accept their fate of a life of insignificant and empty servitude, there are the few that on occasion question the reasons why they do the things we do (but sadly still succumb to their small, predictable calling – the fear of missing out too strong), and then there are the outliers that not just question their menial participation in it all, but act upon it with justification and defiance in the hopes of carving out something more fulfilling. Their only fault waiting for that more fulfilling opportunity to present itself rather than seek it out. And this presently was my most impending dilemma; was this an interlude about to end, or begin? Was I succumbing, failing to act? I didn't know and it gnawed me day and night. What was certain was that a chain of events had begun – the beast in the dark, the tattered book, and now this – and with them a strange and swirling atmosphere was calling them into force for reasons unknown. I left her remark unanswered.

'My apologies, Ms Anderson,' Mr Thompson said walking back into the room, 'where are we up to?'

She looked at me long and patiently; confused, interested, yet at a loss. In quite a casual address I challenged the very structures that got her to where she is today, that gave her a sense of pride and purpose, and yet she doesn't know if I'm crazy, or if there is some truth to it. And now she has no idea what to say next; she wants to re-evaluate her strategy, as they say.

'Ah, actually, we were just finishing up,' she said smiling; forced this time.

'Uh huh,' Mr Thompson mumbled without looking up from his schedule-diary. No time for someone like me. 'Thank you, Bill. That'll be all for now.'

SIX
THIS IS NOTHING NEW

AFTER WORK I CAUGHT THE DOWNTOWN-TRAIN to go see my friend Harvey and unload my irritation with what had transpired at work. Harvey owned and ran *Le Gamaar*: a small, single-screen revival house.[1] He bought or rented and on the odd occasion purloined old 35mm films that studios would otherwise let collect dust in a vault somewhere in Hollywood. With most big theatres going digital, the cost to show movies on film is relatively low. Couple that with regular off-the-books reruns, a film library filled with timeless classics, and at five bucks a ticket, it's no surprise his theatre makes him a tidy living.

And I loved coming here; I loved that a place existed that could survive without surrendering completely to the swinging sword of capitalist greed. Here was a place of business that managed to stay true to the art being offered and the patron paying to see it; there were no Hollywood blockbusters, there was no merchandise to buy, there was no selling out.

For the most part, movie making has finally become wholly an investment industry, not a creative one. Movies are produced by financial backers who want to see more money come back than they lend out; this means that artistic expression is reinterpreted as purely a numbers game for investors. The consumer is offered what is best for the producer, not and never the other way around. This means big budgets for big target audiences; there is no playing room for independent filmmakers with creative scripts and fresh characters anymore.

And people wonder why a ten-cent box of popcorn costs eight bucks, and a six-cent cup of cola runs you another five; mainstream cinemas are forced to squeeze all they can out of the consumer because studios are producing unbelievably expensive films and are cut-throat about ensuring they get their invested return. Meanwhile, the youth of the mainstream are being exposed to a culture of cinema (and most other forms of art) that is abysmal and repugnant, that simplifies story-telling, characterisation, and the verbal expression of human emotion to a stifling and saddening representation. And this is precisely my objection to the common man, to his apathetic understanding and lack of concern in regard to the bleak and pathetic pop culture that he not just allows but perpetuates. Does he not see? Does he not hear? Has man lost the very sense and human touch that drove the deep and powerful Greek tragedies, that inspired Shakespeare's plays, how Mozart conceived the orchestral complexity of his *Requiem Mass in D minor*, or the visions that Da Vinci or van Gogh or Kandinsky tried to harness and embrace in timeless brush strokes of coloured oils that have stunned the creative minds of millions of people over centuries of culture.

We today produce nothing comparable to these great works of art; in our hurry to become successful, or accomplished, or wealthy, we have lost the vision of paradise, we, as receivers of art, have made ourselves blind to the world of magic and the unrushed time it takes to embrace such visionary truths and express them. High art takes effort to appreciate and understand but we have become too tired and too lazy to care; we want to be force-fed our entertainment and with as much car chases, explosions and glittery things as possible.

As I approached the theatre I noticed the marquee read *Fight Club*. Inside, the foyer was small and considerably dated, untouched since Harvey's grandfather's day. The fragrance of fresh popcorn lingered above the soft undertones of old carpet, wood, and dust. Unvarnished brass railings met cracked and peeling cream-painted walls exposing the crumbling redbrick beneath. Decades-old floorboards trodden to a polish creak with welcome from an untold number of filmgoers. A faux-crystal chandelier radiated a dull orangey-yellow glow, and a pair of brown double-doors each with a small circular window marked the entrance to a theatre that seated an intimate one-twenty-five. Inside, old brown leather chairs fit wide and encumbered; their inner cushions stay in perpetual flatness, pressed to an unexpected comfort, like an old pair of slippers you can't bring yourself to throw-out.

I headed upstairs and quietly opened the door to the booth. The projector ticked softly as the reel unwound its stream of still images, displaying the magic of motion picture to our unknowing eye. Harvey was getting ready to do a changeover.

'Hey,' he said softly without looking, getting ready to start the next reel.

I peered through the window: there were maybe thirty, thirty-five people seated (that's a lot for a night's second screening). '*Fight Club*, no wonder you're busy tonight.'

'Yeah,' he said distantly, checking over the projector to make sure the reel spliced smoothly, 'came in last week.'

I plonked down in his chair and stared distantly at the floating dust dancing in the projectors light. Harvey turned around, the projector clicking quietly next to him, 'What's up now?' He said with a smile, knowing me too well.

'You know what I can't stand? The constant bullshit of what the world wants us to be. We work our lives away, why? Because we have to? And what have we got to show for it: a house full of crap, distant memories of a vacation we took too long ago, and a serious lack of sense of self.'

'*Okay*, what brought this on?'

'Tonight, this woman, from HR, starts asking me questions about 'why I work so hard, what I'm doing working here, am I bored?' Of course I'm fucking bored; a monkey could do what I do. But I do it because it pays my tuition; leave it at that. I'm not here to please you or prove myself because of it. Pretend to enjoy coming to this place every day; what does she think I'm going to say?'

'Yeah but most people don't *like* their job, Will.'

'That's precisely my point. *People don't like their job* yet sure enough, they're going to wake up each and every day and waste their lives doing something they don't like. Why? Why do we *really* work?'

'Yes, because we do have to,' Harvey said with a casual laugh. 'The world functions on a monetary system; if you want something you get it through some kind of exchange of goods and services, and money is the backbone of that system. People build their lives around what they're able to do and what it affords them.'

'Wrong. We *need* the system to be an exchange of goods and services. The capitalist system is not designed to raise producers; it was designed to raise consumers. We work not because we want to, hell not even because we need to – not a forty-hour week at least, we work because we've been taught to want to *acquire* things, the more we own the more we feel fulfilled, the better the products, the nicer the car, the bigger the house, the more successful we think we are.'

'Yeah but by not spending, by not *exchanging*, we're robbing someone else of financially prospering. Anyway, that's not all it is. People work as a means to something else, towards something beyond their nine-to-five, they work so they can have other pleasures.'

'Barely. See this is my point,' I stood up and walked over to the window, Pitt was delivering one of the seminal lines of the movie, (I say it with him) "You're not your job. You're not how much money you have in the bank. You're not the car you drive. You're not the contents of your wallet. You're not your fucking khakis'. Right there! He said it over a decade ago, and what's changed? People are still consumers of a life-style obsession; global warming, resource sustainability, education, going to war for profit – people don't care about these things and you know how I can prove it?'

'How?'

'*They're still fucking happening.* We haven't solved anything, we're not replanting forests, we're not preventing climate change, we still spend billions on war efforts, we still drill holes in the earth and burn oil to get from A to B, and we still teach kids to grow up as squares, circles, or triangles while dangling the carrot of 'you can be anything you want kid, you just gotta' work hard at it' in front of their face. Thirty years ago college education was *free*, now it's unaffordable. The government is now encouraging people to get a basic two-year diploma from a community college or learn a trade, why? Because it doesn't want or need a country of intelligent people; it needs a middle-class nation, generations of people that will serve out some menial existence, and contrary to being highly intelligent, analytical, critical thinkers, they'll value what they do because of the basic material things it affords them. And that's what this woman from HR doesn't get; she was implying that the job I do is something more than it is when it isn't.'

I motioned towards the cinema, 'Look at all these people sitting there watching this movie, they've probably seen it half a dozen times by now but I guarantee you each and every one of them is still their college education, still their job, still their fucking khakis. They think they aren't but they are. They think they've moved on but they haven't.'

'You don't think this movie or ones like it changed anyone? Didn't it change you?'

'Yeah but there's a fundamental problem with this film; it didn't offer any resolution. It told us what *not* to be but didn't tell us what *to* be. You may have loved it, like these people obviously did to come back and pay to see it again, but the truth is it leaves you weak in the knees only you can't remember how good the lay was.'

'Go on,' Harvey said, interest peaked.

'Okay, it tells us our idea of happiness has been bought, repackaged, and sold back to us, that we're a culture of brands and products, and that somehow these things should make us feel whole while replacing the more essential pursuit of spiritual happiness. Tick one, thanks Chuck.[2] Two, it probed into the despair and anxiety that people feel ultimately from inheriting this value system that isn't delivering the same meaning and fulfilment it did to previous generations, and yet how many people sitting out there are college grads doing nothing with their education except bestowing upon themselves the ability to critique the futility of this over-consuming culture of which, ironically, they're still contributing to. In fact, the whole Nietzschean *superman*[3] notion is a slap in our face.'

'How so?'

'*Who is Tyler Durden?* He's spontaneous, impulsive, displays an attitude that is seductive and liberating, he's Freud's *id* in all of us – pleasure seeking, full of creation and chaos and charisma, the desire to be free of judgment, of morality, of consequence, but what happens to him? He fucking dies, that's what. His whole existence, although attractively idealistic and dick hardening, doesn't work because who he is has nothing to do with the compromises you and I face in real life.'

'Yeah but that's the catharsis of the film; the changes Ed Norton went through still remain within him. And that's the whole idea of breaking free of our cocoons, to stop being so self-defensive, to throw caution to the wind, to risk failure and become something beyond what we are.'

'And who the fuck does that is what I'm saying? Who do you know lives with those sentiments? Sure, they sound nice and people like pretending that they're living up to such ballsy, stick-it-to-the-man attitudes but are they really? Haven't all these catchcries of Buddhist inspiration or self-empowering motivation just become banal platitudes; said so much and so often that they've become meaningless, or at least forgetting that it takes months or years of effort for the truth of the imparting words to take root. I mean, who saw this movie a decade ago, quit their job the next day and went off to paint self-portraits or build a house in the woods? No one.'

'Well, no shit because you can't just do that. As much as you hate the system, it's the means by which we buy food, clothe ourselves, and put a roof over our head. Yeah, I understand one of your gripes is getting in debt and never escaping, but a lot of people use debt to become something, or do something with their lives.'

'A lot?'

'Well, maybe not a lot. But you're crazy to think that there aren't people out there today who don't see the Western world for what it is, what it's become.'

'Okay, okay, so *some* people might be starting to wake up, see the corruptibility in the world, but we're still starved of opportunity, of place and time to explore, to challenge and express real ideas towards real change; all we have is the illusion of change, the illusion of voice. The so-called democratically elected is really just a popularity contest, and how do candidates increase their popularity? By putting together a pretty damn attractive campaign. But where do they get the money for that? Corporate donations to the tune of hundreds of millions. They use *our* tax dollars to run around the country lying their asses off, making themselves look like champions of our cause only to prevent you, me, and all the other John and Janes out there from really living any better. They just pander to tough times while telling us to keep on keeping-on.'

'So, what are we meant to do?'

'Exactly. And now add to that we're educated, intelligent, and above all else bored. The bottom line is we still largely live within this fraudulent idea of happiness, and worse yet, most people are still chasing it. So, I ask you, did this movie really succeed? Did it really drive home a message usable to generation *whatever* in the twenty-first century?'

'Well, I guess not, at least not to the extent that you're wanting, Will.'

'People may want to be liberated, but they want to do it without sacrifice, and yet without risk there is no reward. Without letting go, how can you discover somewhere new? We hate our government yet we still vote, we're unhappy with the price of gas yet we still drive a car. And what are we really doing, what are we really achieving? Fucking nothing by the dozen. We still follow the old adage of 'work harder to get a better job' so you can spend more money on what? Shit you don't need while the world fucking dies. What are we leaving the next generations?'

'What's wrong, Will? What's really going on? This is

nothing new; we've had this conversation before. Is it Amy? Is it school?'

I waited to respond, searching for a more truthful response than all this complaining, for that's all it was. 'Something is gnawing at me, Harvey, something I've never felt before. My thoughts have taken on a new depth and I guess I'm struggling to make sense of them.'

'Are you going to be okay?'

Only when the walls are caving in do we begin to ask ourselves what's causing it, for it is in grief that we develop the strengths of mind.4 I turned to him and smiled, 'Do we ever really know the answer to such a question?'.

SEVEN
ROPE OVER AN ABYSS

I WENT HOME BUT MY FRUSTRATION SIMMERED; once again finding myself at odds with the falsities and bleakness that society offered me. The difference between Harvey and I was that he made sense of our situation and applied practical responses to our cultural predicament. He was reasonable and always presented a diplomatic response to the dilemmas that I found so great and humiliating to our true potential. And yet, there was probably much in what Harvey said that was true; to compromise one's beliefs in order to make peace with what is wrong so you are able to nurture the aspects that may be right. But this is a compromise I can't make. The well-trodden middle ground is not for me for it is neither hore nor there, it is only half living when we should be fully living. What's more it is the beaten path of the masses, and no treasures shall be found along such known roads.

When I returned to my apartment it was vacant once again, and on my table the *Treatise* beckoned. I took it to the sofa with a head full of pained thoughts; here I was, on the precipice of what I could only see as man's great undoing and poisoned by what it is to bear such knowledge. And perhaps this exposes me more truly, that my life is both unvarnished and shiftless; my situation unbearable and untenable. The only answer, why, death of course. To end my detested view of the world the sword must be thrust, and thrust by my own hand... unless, forged in the depths of a renewed self-knowledge, I underwent a transformation and passed over to a new and undisguised self; a metamorphosis of thought, orientation and purpose.

And yet such a transition is not unknown or uncommon to me; I had often experienced it already and always in times of utmost despair. During these terribly uprooting journeys into the plumbed depths of my psyche, the self I had grown to know was shattered wholly and completely. On each occasion powers of a deep and forgotten origin had struck the innermost core of myself, as it then was, and destroyed it; and each time entire aspects of myself would be lost that were formerly loved and cherished, and finally above all else, true to me no more.[1]

And it was happening again. This hateful vacancy, this deathly stillness of loneliness and disconnection always preceded the sudden and painful stripping of personal ideals and beliefs such as I was enduring now, to pass through once again.[2] *For so long as there is something I can do about it, I am not yet dead,[3] I have not yet completely lost my life.* And in this emptiness, this lovelessness and despair of which I find myself, it shall be found, a self-knowledge brought forth from the depths, imbued with a truth and knowledge beyond the reach of culture or convention.

That was the dream, the beast in the dark, and now of course this little tattered book; it was all pointing the direction... I held the book in my hands, it feeling stranger than before, and started turning its yellowed pages. Before long I was filled with a sense of awe and puzzlement, even vindication for my spiteful and weary ways. Here was written the testament of my soul, of my thoughts and desires, of my destitution at this very moment. But how was it so true, so accurate in its portrayal of me? How could something so old speak with such union and exactness? It was like reading a memoir of my personal ideals, but also an instruction manual for how to continue living this lonely and removed life. It was as wonderful as it was shocking.

As I sat reading on the sofa the moon drifted across the night's sky and constellations came and went. The hour was late and I was dreary; not from lack of sleep but from the flood of knowledge for my known situation. This *Treatise* had no author, no publication stamp, no date, nor signature. It was but a leather and paper looking-glass filled with the dislocation of my personal plight in the here and now. It filled me with an extreme strangeness, a déjà vu like nothing I had felt before. It had confirmed in me the knowledge that indeed something was missing in my life, but that that something must be known to me for how else would I know it to be absent. What's more it tells of my internal division, my split, not just with society and its common man but with *myself*; like a shattered mirror there are a thousand shards and a thousand selves eager to live a thousand lives; hardly two, least of all one. And to heed its warning that it is a curse to become aware of the thousand-self soul for society is incapable of recognising this divine truth, and so, the lonely wolves become gravely misunderstood by the herd, and are cast out. Tragically, all individuals exist in this state but fail to plumb the depths of their inner self and instead of finding a cosmic ocean of knowledge and potential, they find in its place a ruling ego that feeds on the most basic of pleasures,[4] and so hand themselves over for a few morsels of momentary delight in the otherwise immorality and dimness which they have the gall to call living.

In delirium my head swum, but still I turned its pages and absorbed its words. At last, when my mouth was dry and my eyes ached, I turned the last of the yellowed pages. And its intimate knowledge of my weary state of ways was because I was not the only one; indeed there are those that came before me as well as those that shall come after, born at a time not right for them and destined to live a lonely life of lovelessness and despair.[5] Their life's journey wrought with peril until they reach the calling of their destiny, and the mark they leave on the world everlasting. And the thing that is unknown is the unique and particular life-goal of the person – their purpose for living one of their thousand lives; how they reach this boon is by travelling along the path of their true destiny, should they heed its call and choose to accept it, for such gifts are not to be grasped without venturing beyond the walls of tradition and consciousness.

Yet, in that moment I reflected and stumbled upon a fault in the nihilistic sermon the beast in the dark tenderly gave, and within this book he claimed would bear the answers to my woes. But even he, the now meek beast, could not transgress his humanist self to become wholly wolf (or nihilist) that he so wanted to be; his seething fury only shows for what was missed in his day.

No, my dear wolf, we exist in the world of *becoming*, not the thing become. And to compare oneself to wolf is to paint a very bleak picture for man *and* wolf. In certain respects the wolf is superior to man for it has not yet made itself conflicted by blundering into a consciousness or for that matter pitted an unscrupulous self-willed ego against the cosmic beauty and power from which it belongs. Were the wolf conscious it would be morally better than man.[6] To say we are civilised and look at our greatness is an embarrassing assertion (for one only needs to look around let alone at our past to bear witness to the horror we have unveiled to the world). And, as the *Treatise* suggests, to say there are those that are wolves and look at their purity to live as they must, and should, is too calling an end to what is yet to be greater, calling an end to the *becoming* but saying *aha!* Look at what I have become.

Despite the hour I went up to the rooftop, to the cold, night air that I always found so refreshing; the moon glowed ghostly from behind a patched curtain of soft cloud, my breath steaming in long plumes. I wondered where he was now, that man, that beast... that phantom of the night. A police siren sounded, somewhere far away; *is that you*, I wondered, lurking through the darkness to plague another poor soul only it didn't go so well? Maybe I could come looking for you, tell you that you were wrong, that there was an error in your ways; that there was more to it, something beyond your foresight.

He told me I am a wolf amongst sheep, but for what gain? If we are to overcome ourselves then we are not to remain the beast within or succumb to our self-imposed slavery. We must be more than we are, we must create beyond ourselves! We must move forward, and to be wolf is to return to a time we have already left behind. No, our future does not lie in nourishing our inner wolf, or ape, for we are always moving forward, towards more and more increased states of consciousness. We are forever in the process of becoming rather than that which has become. We cannot unlearn what we have learned about nature, or about ourselves. He spoke of immortals, well I have one for him, his name is Nietzsche, and he spoke thus: 'Man is a rope, fastened between animal and *superman* – a rope over an abyss. What is great in man is that he is a bridge and not a goal.'[7]

A cruel breeze blew and pulled at my clothes. But what if the book was a key and not the answer? If the entrance to the cave has made itself visible, then it is I who must lift the veil and step into that darkness, that abyss where the immortals live on.

Beyond the city, the dark towers that gleamed and glittered, and beyond the ranges further off, the world was curving and dawn painted her approach; stars faded at her coming and blacks turned to blues. I realised I was shivering and went back down to my apartment; my mind a tangled mess of exhausted contemplation. A strange night and day and now night again; peculiar; cosmic; the universe conspiring.

A new day was soon arriving, just as it did for *Zarathustra*; 'Great star! What would your happiness be, if you had not those for whom you shine!'[8] I laughed deliriously, thinking of Nietzsche, and then a spark; I rummaged my book stacks for this very masterpiece. Finding it (*Thus Spoke Zarathustra*), I flicked through its pages rapaciously, looking for some passage, a particular passage, a passage that I could only remember for the feeling that welled inside me as I flicked its pages and its words drew near. My mouth was a desert from excitement; I stood in front of the bay window, dawn breaking, and with serendipity striking I held the book open to what I had read a dozen times before but by pure providence struck me so fatally on this fateful morning: 'I teach you the *superman*. Man is something that should be overcome. What have you done to overcome him? All creatures hitherto have created something beyond themselves: and do you want to be the ebb of this great tide, and return to the animals rather than overcome man? What is the ape to men? A laughing-stock or a painful embarrassment. And just so shall man be to the *superman*.'[9]

I fell onto the sofa, breathless and dizzy. Tears welled and a smile creased my mouth. The thing that gnawed the pit of my stomach had cracked like a seed. Something ever so small had been awakened.

EIGHT
WHERE DO I FIT IN?

I SLEPT ALL DAY AND DREAMED DREAMS that gave me goose bumps and shivers. When I awoke, I re-read the *Treatise*, and re-read *Zarathustra*. I let the loftiness of ideas swim inside my head, and felt exuberance and wonder, but also, painfully, still quite contained – not quite trapped, but rendered incapable to act, somehow. I couldn't explain this feeling even to myself; as though I wanted to speak but had no mouth, as though I wished to paint but had no hands, as though I longed to hear music played, a violin perhaps, but there was no violinist.

I put those thoughts aside and went to visit Amy that evening. As I sat on the train I relived the night in the alleyway over and over; relived the beast in the dark, his voice, his words; relived dawn breaking and for the first time deeply feeling Nietzsche's words, those words I'd read before. By the time I arrived at Amy's apartment, I was filled with such a renewed sense of vigour, such excitement and bewilderment. I was in such fervour; splendid deliriousness; crazed wonder; a sudden thirst for living had parched me so deeply that no mortal potion could quench it.

When I arrived I spoke in streams, trying miserably to explain the moment of clarity that dawned on me the night just passed. But all Amy could question was, 'Who was this man? Why were you talking to a beggar? What book, why would you take such a thing?' It was all her fear and caution and prudence for the unknown, her socially conditioned instruction to avoid such undesired situations; and naturally, missing entirely the importance of what I was saying. Forever getting caught up on the insignificant trivialities and irrelevant details that no longer mattered for they were now in the past and to explain them would be to rob me of the bounty of this moment.

Whatever I was trying to say to Amy was evidently inarticulate and obscure and scared her. I was suddenly, at this late hour, full of energy, energy that she had been longing for, the passion and desire, but I was much more than that. I was a fireball of untempered thought aching to explode into some kind of physical manifestation; something still unknown to me I realised.

I looked around her apartment, seeing things for the first time that I had seen a hundred times before; the cursively carved block of wood that read 'beautiful life' on the bookshelf, the framed picture of 'keep calm and chase your dreams' next to the other framed stencil art of 'this is the beginning of anything you want.' *Are you? Is it, really?* The *Vanity Fair* coffee table book, the vase full of plastic lemons, bronze Buddha statue, apple seed rosary wrapped around a ceramic hand on a stand giving the peace symbol. I felt foreign and lost.

We somehow got onto the topic of love. 'The sublime! That is what is behind love! Beyond it! Love is just an idea, a construct, not a thing in itself to be held,' I lamented poetically. 'This is our mistake; to conceive of love as though it is something set, something exact. It is not meant to be fully understood, fully known. Only knowledge can be understood because it can be defined. Love cannot be defined for it is different for everyone. Do you see? Love should be simpler, something you feel without needing to explain it.'

'I see how you look, how you feel when you read *Dostoyevskee, Tergeneif, Nietchee*; when you describe art to me. That is love, maybe love for this 'sublime', but it is still love. And I can feel it, feel what's not there. You don't truly love me, not enough, not in the way you should... in the way you're meant to.'

It was true I suddenly realised. I could not love (the way she wanted me to) another human being who was so simple, so unaware, always fussing about, shifting – yes, but only from one dismal pole to another. Not true shiftlessness that I could admire, not true vagrancy, or true transformation of the self. No, the common man goes through all but a safe and cosy maturation; sure he claims to have his heart broken once or twice, sure he claims to be stressed by work or money or friendship – but none of this is on the cutting board of living or dying! He knows not what anything absolute is; just the broad meadow of summer grass with its farmer and fence to keep the foxes out, and warm apple pies resting on the windowsill.

'You are so full of shit.' She said, tears welling.

No, the world is so full of shit, and it is my constant shiftlessness and curiosity and bewilderment that are real. People live their lives in a limited number of ways, boxes; one for home, one for work, and one for entertainment. And inside these boxes are very pacified and specific ways to act and behave and think even. When you behave appropriately you are rewarded, and when you behave negatively you get punished. Every day and every week we move with absolute predictability between these three cages, and we surrender to this way without even realising. We do not change or grow or see the world with new eyes. How can we when the view is always the same.

'To love is to appreciate,' I went on, 'and to appreciate is to be able to regard from afar after experiencing, after growing. To truthfully grow or change you must let go of who you are, let go of what you define as real or right or familiar; a risk most find utterly incomprehensible.'

'And what about me, where do I fit into that pretty little phrase? Will you be letting go of me?' Her face a picture of pain.

This was a regular problem that tormented me: these nuances of insecurity, the referring of everything back to her, the whittling down of perhaps glorious and all likely momentary ideas as though we were talking about specific details of our relationship. You cannot build a home on sand and at this very moment I am less than sand; I am dust. Disappearing more and more was the fascinated audience which she once gave me, gave my sudden fountains of thought and insight. Instead, more often she replaced it with misconstrued and misunderstood attacks towards her; towards us.

And then, all too often I was incapable of saying what she wanted to hear, mostly because I was talking about something else entirely, and I would be too frustrated to bring the notion down, reduce it to the level that hurt her, and so her hurt feelings remained open wounds. Was it wrong of me to leave things like that? To not comfort her, her own undoing and self-confusion? She wanted a happy life so badly, but to know true happiness you must go through true pain. And perhaps this was it, perhaps her shimmering ideal of love needed to be dinted by despair in order to know what real is.

I left her apartment and was saddened at the thought that it may be me, and this relationship, that would teach her this painful lesson about life. I wondered then, what I was learning from it, this interlude. To create beyond oneself is to perish, and perhaps that is what I needed to go through.

NINE
A LOFTY SPEECH

THE NEXT DAY AT WORK, much to the squint-eyed fury of my bellyaching manager, I was called back into the office for another meeting.

'Hello, Will.' Sally said warmly; she was happy to see me, happy for a fresh start. She was professional but in a kind, affable sort of way. And above all else she was the HR manager; hardly the type of person with a preference for confrontation.

'Hello, Ms Anderson,' I said amicably.

'Will, I have been with this company for seven years, and in that time I have seen many types of people. I've also moved a lot of good people around; given them opportunities to become something far greater than what they were when they first walked in. But in those seven years no one has spoken to me the way you did.' Her tone was honest, hopeful. She liked herself because of the shot at success she could give someone, not realising it was entirely within them in the first place, and it was the system that held them back.

'So,' she continued, 'I hope you can understand why, after our first meeting, I wanted to find out a little more about you.' She smiled again, her call sign. 'How come you didn't say that you had been to college?'

'Because I didn't think it was irrelevant.'

She began to look over some files in front of her; her face growing in bewilderment. 'Psychology, social studies, philosophy... economics, marketing...' She looked up at me wildly curious, 'You have one semester to go, why don't you finish? I mean your qualifications, your GPA; you could be *extremely* successful.'

I sighed. 'No, I could be extremely productive.'

'*Why* are you working here, Will?'

'Because I'm forced to, Ms Anderson. I am *forced* to work here.' We stared at each other; the space between us full of tension. 'What do you want from me?'

'What do I want?' The blue of her eyes bright and bewildered. 'I want to offer you a promotion, Will.'

I shook my head, suddenly waking up to the nonsense. 'You think that's what I want? You think that's what I need?'

'I-I don't understand?' Her face a mess of confusion.

'You don't understand that I don't want to work for the next forty years? That an impending global financial collapse will evaporate any retirement I may accumulate? You don't understand that in order to cheer myself up from a life of endless menial work – which I'll tell myself isn't menial – I have to buy myself things I don't want or need? Then convince myself that these soon-to-be out-dated material possessions will somehow bring me happiness and fulfilment. Or maybe they'll just make me fit in, make me feel like I belong and have something in common with all the other people sold the same lie, feel connected, liked, maybe get a well-to-do girlfriend out of it? Succumb to status anxiety because despite having a house full of possession I still feel hollow on the inside, read some self-help crap by some uppity MD who can tell me exactly what I need to hear but is a generation behind the eight-ball, so ultimately their 'eight-steps to enlightenment for the modern person' falls on deaf ears. I can listen to Jimmy but I can't hear him. And instead of asking myself why I feel so empty I'll just turn to the next best solution: *reality television* because somehow watching other people be stupid makes me feel better about my miserable life. Flat-screen, tablet, smartphone; so long as I have these I'm a part of the have's right? That is until China decides to stop building them for a tenth of what they really cost, but so long as my kid isn't the one missing out on an education or going blind putting it together, what do I care? And for what at the end of the day? So I can value myself in some ignorant and sadistic way? When in truth all I'm really doing is perpetuating a cycle of gross consumerism and pursuing valueless endeavours in order to fulfil a culturally constructed idea of happiness. Be good, be moral, go to college, get a good job, buy a car, buy a house, get *really* in debt, and maintain the status quo for the rest of my mostly depressed life?

'But I won't tell myself that, in fact I won't even ask myself the very questions that'll lead to that soul-destroying realisation. I'll just pay three-fifty for a cup of coffee everyday so I'm productive at work, ignoring the thirty-cents a day pay-cheque the person is earning to pick the Arabica slow-roasted beans so some trans-national ten-thousand miles away can turn an eight-figure profit while paying its employees minimum wage.

And then I'll just drink my sorry ass into a coma on weekends not because I can't bear the thought of work on Monday let alone every Monday for the next decade, but because that choice somehow eludes itself from existence in this 'so-called' abundant and free society. And even if I wanted stop, go on a life-journey of some description, I can't because it's too late, I've already bought into this reality, this story, I've already committed myself too much and for too long that it's easier to *not* question what I'm doing or why I'm doing it, accept my fate, work hard, impress my manager, hope to get a promotion, and make sure I thank God for making it so good.

'But the burning question is: whose status quo am I really propping up and for how long? The already wealthy or the growing underclass needed to feed the system? Have we simply forgotten about poverty, unemployment, education, racial or gender discrimination? Or have I just been gently nudged onto other pressing social and environmental issues that I still lack any backbone to do anything about; global warming, forest degradation, civil wars in the Middle East, terrorist propaganda, these are the things that now motivate me but only so much as that I don't actually have to do anything about. When in reality what's really happened is that I've been cleverly distracted from trying to motivate change for myself and the immediate cycle to which I perpetuate.'

I was on fire then, and continued unabated, 'How about you, you're upper-middle probably earning one-fifty, eat organic, drive a hybrid so you can say you're doing your part for the environment. Too bad you're twenty-nine-ninety-nine bottle of shampoo contributes to mass deforestation and the extinction of who knows how many species of animals, but as far as you're concerned it's worth it because even I can smell how good it is from across the table. But it's not all bells and whistles right, you pay your taxes, donate to charity, you don't go to church anymore but you used to, and that still counts, right? At least you're concerned about global warming and the effect the ever-increasing price of oil has on the economy, only you're still pro-War on terror not realising the two go hand-in-hand. You're committed to your job because you've still got a mortgage, and that makes you feel honest and hardworking; but you've probably got a second home or even a third, or maybe a holiday house somewhere overlooking a nice private beach or an acre of pristine woodland by your back door.

Meanwhile, a quarter of the country doesn't own a home and two-thirds will never pay-off the one they do have. Am I close?'

She looked assaulted, or at least threatened. Her eyes were wide and scared; her brow scrunched in anguish. All of a sudden the peculiar interest she showed in wanting to know more about me has turned out to be something offensive. She was no longer impressed or fascinated by this mysterious and intriguing young man before her, just scared.

Noticing her hand I continued, 'The fact of the matter is you've just turned forty-something, you've got too much career success and you're far too good looking to not have been married, which means you're divorced. Am I right?'

She said nothing but her face betrayed her. Her mouth was agape, and her eyes filled with hurt. I lowered my tone, speaking softer, gentler; this wasn't personal, it was just a matter of fact.

'So you married for career, for financial luxury. How'd that workout for you? And you're asking me why it doesn't make sense that I don't want the same thing, that I don't want to fall for the same trap? Be pushing forty, going through a divorce because I suddenly realise

I have no fucking idea who I am and yet I have an uncontrollable need to reclaim myself by banging the neighbours teenage daughter in the back of my European four-wheel-drive. I mean we all *think* we know who we are; that's what plugging myself into this little pantomime tells me, doesn't it?'

I sighed.

'The system doesn't care about me, it doesn't even care about you. I mean you've worked it pretty good and for that and those like you I congratulate you, but the problem still remains, even you in all your career success still wonder who you really are, think about the doors you didn't open that maybe should have, and when on those lonely nights you feel like crying to yourself for reasons you don't quite know, well this is why. You came from a generation that chose functionality over actuality; and now the reoccurring question of 'why my life lacks meaning and purpose' weighs on your chest and you haven't the faintest idea how to get rid of it.

'You're giving me an opportunity that'll change my life, right here, right now. And if I take it my life will never be the same. I will be able to afford more things, more comforts, better tasting food, and probably a better class of life; that's true. But at what cost? And to who?

And here in lies the illusion; I can get a nice car, I can get a mortgage on a decent house, and I can have a five to ten year plan for working my way up the next few rungs on the corporate ladder; and while I'm at it, I'll wave goodbye to the next twenty years of my life. And what will I have to show for it but two weeks' vacation each year, a house full of stuff, and financial debt that will stop me from doing anything but work for the next forty years. The dream doesn't sound so dreamy when you say it like that does it?'

She didn't reply; she had nothing to say. She understood what I was saying but life had not garnered her with any answers that would remotely satisfy the ideological barrage I threw at her. This was beyond her, her generation, her mindset that had followed the rules and stayed the course to live a happy little life that wasn't so happy after all.

'Or, I don't take the promotion. Better yet, I quit, right here, right now. Production goes down one- maybe two-percent for a few days, you have the new guy start Monday because there's that many people out on their ass looking for work, and this place, this company forgets all about me. Like I never existed.

'And you want me to be happy about that

arrangement? Be grateful, be proud of myself that I worked so hard for you, this company, to grant me this opportunity? That my efforts here are somehow what makes me worthwhile, gives my life purpose, meaning, for what? So a bunch of old rich guys can get richer while you pay me just enough for me to stick my head in the sand and admire what I see. No fucking thanks.

'Make no mistake about it; a promotion is a promise, a promise to never be free. And I'm not talking about putting daisies in my hair, smoking a peace pipe, and dancing in a field under a double rainbow. I'm talking about the freedom of choice, to follow a path that I believe, that I find worthwhile, one that I can get on and off or change entirely without the threat of financial bankruptcy. At least something that doesn't rope me in fifty hours a week, slowly make me forget about what I actually used to want to be, realise that my youth has all but slipped away, and all of a sudden I've turned into a bitter, old, conservative prick because I only care about me and what's mine, and I don't want my taxes going to some bum who's not willing to work a day in his life like I had to suck up and do.

'That's a tough realisation to have but once you have it you'll never look at the world the same again.

Every job, every deadline, every time your boss asks you to work overtime you'll think to yourself, 'Why? What difference will it make... what difference am *I* making?' And the answer is none.

'Some people don't want to ask themselves that, most won't even think to ask, because the answer is too crippling; that the very reason you get up every morning and will get up every morning for at least the next twenty or thirty or forty years is to perform a pointless job that although *anyone* could do, you find some personal meaning in, some unique yet deluded drive that gives your life definition, as though you should start determining *who you are* from that point forward. 'Hi, my name is so-and-so, I'm a fucking who gives a shit.' Or worse yet, squeeze who you really are or really want to be somewhere between your eight to ten-hour work day with an hour commute on either side, grocery shopping, bad reality television, doing the laundry, masturbating, and the crap sleep you get before you've got to be up at six-am to do it all over again. That'll give you depression, but not the fact we live in a world where thirty-thousand children under the age of five die every day.'

I stood up, proud, thirsty, dizzy.

'Are you not more than that?' I asked rhetorically.

'Are we not all more than that?'

What a whirlwind. I said all I wanted to say, all I needed to say; as much as for her as for myself.

Ms Anderson was shell-shocked.

'Then again, if we all thought this way, who'd do the jobs nobody else wanted to do?'.

TEN
THE MEDIOCRE TRAGEDY

'What happened after that?'

'I said, 'thanks but no thanks. I quit'. And walked out of there.'

Harvey looked at me speechless.

'What? The world is full of artists, Harvey. And musicians and writers and inventors and explorers – they just don't know it, they gave it up to be something they're not, to do something anybody could do.'

'Shh, keep your voice down,' Harvey said getting up to look out the projectionist's window.

I had gone straight to *Le Gamaar* from work, my place of refuge, and of course Harvey being the only one I could talk to.

'That's all well and good, Will, but that's not how things work. Not now, not today.'

'Then when?' I said hotly. 'Toffler said, 'The illiterate of the twenty-first century will not be those who cannot read and write, but those who cannot learn, unlearn, and relearn.'[1] And what a world we live in; so set in its ways, so sure of itself, and people so sure of it.'

'Look, I agree with you, *fundamentally*, but life is about compromise. It's about juggling what we have to do with what we enjoy doing. Not everyone is destined or capable of being an artist or a musician or a writer or anything of those things. Yes, *maybe*, in the future, societies won't be so overgrown, that maybe there'll be a gradual decaying of the mega-city and with the aid of technology and renewable resources we will have fully self-supporting communities that don't need to be a part of a sprawling metropolis. Then, yes, perhaps in that will there be the availability and freedom to spend more time pursuing the things that we have a love or interest for. But the sad and very real truth is that is not here, not now, not today.'

'And I'm saying compromise is a nice way of putting up with things that aren't right. The system *is* breaking; it's just not broken *yet*. If you see it for what it io, how can you accept being a contributing part of it? And isn't that the problem, there's no alternative, no trade-off for those who think differently, want to express themselves differently; they're caught between two worlds. We live two lives; one where we work, chained to our computers or our cell phones or our cash register, told how to live our lives, what to aim for, what to like, what to feel. And the other is in our dreams, in those moments lost in thought wishing we were somewhere else doing something different, feeling happy, free, connected to something, to someone. But we're not; we're stuck, caught-out, we've been lead down a path of guarantees only to realise that it leads somewhere else.'

'Where?'

'Fucking nowhere that's where. The developed world is producing graduates faster than the economy can produce jobs, and there's no place to put them. And if it's happening now, it's only going to keep happening. It boggles the mind how people can still follow the herd, embrace this given way of going through life that is absolutely guaranteed to either destroy the world or us in the process.'

I took a breath, 'Look, I don't want to be a college grad, or a labourer, or a corporate sell-out, Harvey, because the first is nothing with the allusion of being something, the second is soul-destroying monotony, and the third is a trap for a hollow existence of superficial and material waste.'

'Yeah but you can't say you're an example of the system failing when you haven't failed at it yet, Will.'

'*Yet*. Exactly. I don't need to try and fail to prove that it's broken. Even if I tried and succeeded the system would *still* be broken, Harvey. That's what successful people don't get; just because you made it doesn't mean the world is peachy, that if everyone just did it the way you did no one would have anything to complain about. Everyone would be happy. As though the relentless churning of the capitalist machine would somehow run on its own good merit, not realising that it requires an underclass to keep the coal fires burning, and that the insatiability of Western culture is creating more social and environmental problems than it's solving. And the only way to keep the lower class happy is to give them just enough that they think they're part of the have's instead of the have not's. Meanwhile, ship the really shit jobs off-shore to some proper underclass of people from a country most people can't find on a map because those poor sons-of-bitches don't know what health care, holidays, or a disposable income is, and 'exploitation' is a word they'll never learn.'

I tempered my reproach, my venting mostly over, 'No. I'm jumping ship before we hit the iceberg. I know we're going down, I'm just not going to play along filling myself with false hope and delusion about the job I got having some grand purpose or it being the formula for a perfect life.'

We were quiet for a moment before Harvey shifted the conversation. 'Why are you taking aim so strongly at the common man? Society, culture, it does change, yes, quite slowly, but there *are* movements all over the world working towards a better future: non-government organisations, charities, political and environmental groups, *people*. They're out there.'

I thought deliberately before giving my answer. 'I'm taking aim at the common man because he is everywhere, he is the majority, he ultimately drives the fate of the world, and he is oblivious.'

I stood up and looked through the small window, watching people's faces flicker and glow in the light of the film; quiet, passive, unaware.

I turned back to Harvey, 'And here's why: the tragedy of the common man's culture is not obvious like the exploding of bombs or starving children or the *truly* enslaved labour working for cents a day, but it is still there, hidden in plain view. The tragedy, Harvey, is *mediocrity*; it is wasted days of pointless fussing. 'Oh I must wash my car, oh but the oven needs a clean, oh I must tidy up the garage, oh what exotic dish should I make my dinner guests, oh the big game is on, oh let us meet at the bar and drink the day away,' and so on. One could argue bleakly that these are the fruitful realities of living in a fortunate and comfort rich society, that this *is* what one is meant to do with their 'days off.' But is it not heartbreakingly obvious they prevent one from using leisure time on things of greater value, of more significance, towards things of deeper fulfilment? For themselves *or* for their fellow man? Contemporary life almost completely neglects the effective use of leisure. We live in a marvellous time of communication and technology, of self-expression and opportunity to self-express, and yet what the vast majority of us do with our free time are scarcely things we can be proud of. And the common retort is this: 'I can do whatever I want with my free time,' or 'I am allowed to enjoy these simple activities, who are you to judge?' Not realising that they are the sad excuses one uses precisely because they have *no other activity* which garners them even a whiff of deeper fulfilment or a more spiritual happiness.'

I was lost, lost in the pain and suffering and melancholy I feel for, and on behalf of, my fellow man. That was the truth. We have failed; so long as people suffer, so long as we support a society that allows people to lose themselves, to not become something proud and fulfilling and of their own volition, we have failed.

My mood became sombre. 'So many years have disappeared, Harvey. Doing what? I've forgotten so many of them that it can only mean so very little was gained. Isn't that regrettable? To live this life once and yet to fill it with so much boredom and tedium – how dare we. I'll never have those warm nights back, that youthful lust for adventure, that energy to carry on past sleepless nights spent laying somewhere, drunk on life, staring up at the stars. I can only regret them now, regret their dullness, their lifelessness, that nothing monumental was done with them. Because, really, what have I gained since? Very little I suppose. Condemned by our own bleak impoverishment and be thankful for a mediocre life.

'Where does the honest living come from, the honest sensation of feeling something real or new or exciting that shakes or inspires you? It's not just the mediocrity that is modern society's tragedy but its predictable and practiced and well thought-out lives. And when life is predictable it surely ceases being life. And isn't it the more surely and vividly we know the future, the more it makes sense to say that you've already had it, Harvey?'[2]

ELEVEN
VALLEY OF DEATH

I ASKED HARVEY TO GO WITH ME and find a small, quiet bar, preferably unfrequented and solemn, so that we could drink unobtrusively in our own company; and not for leisure but for the purpose of revelry. He laughed at my proposal and said, 'but you don't drink!' Which was true, but I had stolen myself away that night, torn loose the shackles of the job I detested and felt the sublime shiver of one's liberation from a deplorable internment such that a celebration was in order.

We got drunk very quickly. My hasty departure from the den of the bellyachers meant the night was still early; and already we were full of cheap wine without a mouthful of dinner to accompany it. As my head swam, I expressed all sorts of embarrassment and regret at the manner of my resignation. It was lofty and patronising and all too proud – proud in a pompous self-righteous kind of way (as though I was so sure of myself which, I assure you, I am not). I felt exalted by it too though, that was honestly speaking. I am far from perfect, I know that, and that poor woman – I laughed shamefully – I berated myself for the attack on her (who was she?), but it wasn't really her, just what she symbolised and stood for.

'She would probably forget it all in a few days, wouldn't she?' I said to Harvey, asking as much as answering. He agreed.

We sank more wine. My audience may have only been one but the proclamation was a turning point (it *was* something beautiful), a brief moment of self-actualising, a growl, a dagger, a rebuke. No! *A calling into reality the very opportunities we must carve for ourselves as we respond to the call of our true destiny.* I laughed manically. The thing that was known but unknown was closer than it once was; I could taste its sweetness behind the fermented crushed grapes that I swashed and spilt as we rambled in our merriment.

Enough of all that; that was all in the past now, and we had more pressing things to discuss. I confessed to

Harvey that I had accepted a gift from an unknown man, a beast, and that reading it perhaps ignited the fire for this self-approved right with which I now imbued myself. I confessed to its prophetic nature, to its calling, its persuasion to become aware of what we are. I was too drunk (I put down my wine) to explain with succinctness its almost biblical quality. Instead, I could only express the deep emotion that welled inside me; covering my face with melancholic hands and then suddenly blearing with finger pointed in the air, saying such things as: 'Yes! Man is a many sided die except he sees only one, the fool!' And, 'We call ourselves civilised and yet we are so callow; we call ourselves enlightened and yet we fear to ask ourselves who we are! And live accordingly to that sweet virtue of self-knowledge.'

We soon left the bar; its glumness perforated by a group of charming young men in suits and their obnoxious gossiping and laughter. The night was dark and the cold air bit right to our bones. Arm-in-arm we stumbled onto the main street that was aglow with fashion stores, restaurants, fancy bars, a movie theatre, and an ice-creamery. A paved parade for the bourgeois to bask in the frivolous luxury of their fruitful toiling.

Everyday people passed us doing their everyday

things; oblivious to our drunken state in the middle of the week; a night not appropriate for drunkenness, and yet the very same drunkenness they would most likely participate in a night or two from now. Cars shuffled noisily on the street, honking and squeezing their way through in a mad rush to get their occupants home; eager for their nightly dose of bad reality television, warm clichéd regard for one another, and finally that insufferable sigh of *'I don't want to'* – referring to the contract they signed with their blood and spirit whereby they donate the majority of their life in return for a comparatively mediocre sum of money.

Our jovial indirection brought us to one of those twenty-four-hour gyms; 'Ha!' I said to Harvey. Its occupants on display in the front window for passer-byes to see, to be drawn in, to be attracted to, or made to feel sad and jealous, reflecting miserably that they aren't on the same road to physical perfection that those people are clearly on. A hobby of self-obsessed ruin when one becomes addicted, when no use becomes of it. Swept up, caught in the web of physically objectifying themselves (and all those around them by unconscious comparison), and perpetuating a noxious and delusional cultural trap that to have an underwear model body is to attain some personal or social value, that once 'there' you are now worth something to someone, not realising that they too (the persons of similar interests that you're trying to allure) are just as superficial and hypercritical in their ideals of body image. All the while not seeing that, for the most part, it's just the net result of one's genetics pushed to an obsessive and narcissistic end for a shallow and fleeting fulfilment.

'Ego-boosting!' I yelled at no one in particular.

And is it such a surprise that man feels the need to boost his stifled ego in this sedated and emasculated society? He is losing touch with his proud self (which one should) but not through effortful introspection and the understanding of letting go of his false self, an identity constructed for him; instead, it's being taken from him, and now he seeks out appropriate and socially acceptable means to inflate and parade himself, to reclaim his prowess in a show of pseudo-homoerotic and narcissistic leisure time.

'There! Is that man and everything he should or could be? Is he not regressing? Is there nothing better he could be doing with his life? Is there nothing better he *wants* to do with his life?' I asked Harvey forlornly.

'Such a pageantry of vanity!' He intoned.

We laughed manically, still slightly inebriated.

'No, no, but it's not, Harvey. Do you know what I see? I see a cry for help; a cry to be something of value in this shallow world, except they're pursuing an activity that only perpetuates the disease.'

'Say that again,' Harvey said with drunken confusion.

'You see, the generation before us valued material possessions and conspicuous consumption because it meant that you had succeeded at life, it meant status amongst your peers, respect, even envy, but ultimately it meant happier lives because you owned the very *things* that promised it. The industrial revolution moved from the factory floor and entered our homes – televisions, microwave ovens, a thirty-two-piece knife set; the new world of door-to-door salesmen, infomercials, and advertising companies exploded into our lives and your family wasn't keeping up with the Jones's unless you had whatever the latest and greatest was. *This* was your measure of success and happiness in twentieth-century modern society. Households chartered themselves to accumulating as many gizmos and gadgets and as much bankable wealth as they could; bigger houses with bigger yards, swimming pools and outdoor barbeques; new dresses and golf clubs, bikes for the kids, remote-control cars and barbie dolls, only to be tossed away or forgotten about after minimal use. And they did this because they thought that, surrounded by such material prosperity and social status, their children would grow up happy and well-adjusted and go become doctors and lawyers and presidents and freakin' astronauts.

'But all this created was a generation of kids who would become superficial and materialistic; and it created this because they got everything they wanted without having to work for it. Look around us,' I began to point at various business, 'clothing store, clothing store, jewellery store, gym, designer bags, designer shoes, hair salon, beauty salon, 'everything on this street is geared towards making yourself look outwardly attractive. We ignore the diffused anxiety and intermittent flashes of sheer unhappiness that grip at the core of who we are because we don't know how to deal with it. We think we need a holiday or a change of job or a new outfit, but these are only temporary fixes. The person addicted to the gym is no different to the goth with spikey hair, the girl who spends her pay-cheque on new clothes, or the guy with the sleeve tattoo; they're all just arbitrary attempts to express ourselves and the want to feel special in today's society.'

'So, what are we really after?' Harvey asked.

'Good question. What are people really chasing? The home appliances, the flashy new car, the underwear model body? No, no, no. What people really want is a sense of value; what they're lacking is self-esteem, and we're so lacking in it because our parents got sold the wrong way to achieve it and they unwittingly passed it onto us. And here's the kicker; underserved praise and the promise of material prosperity became the backbone of the generation that got it all handed to them; it has rendered the psyche full of unjustified entitlement, and not just to material things – cars, laptops, smartphones, but more importantly to a certain way of life – privilege, opportunity, and above all else, happiness.

'The superficial world that gross materialism created is crumbling after only one or two generations; the world is rife with the vain and narcissistic but underneath vanity and narcissism is really a cry to be heard, a desire to be validated on an individual level for something, acknowledged for something; it is our deeper drive for self-esteem and self-worth manifesting as behaviour that attracts social attention, even if that attention is for nothing worthwhile.'

'Mmm.'

'Look, we know that the higher our self-esteem the happier we are, yet we still live in a world that values your civic function over what you actually offer humanity, or how good looking you may be over how intelligent or talented you actually are. When we strive to do something better, we eventually succeed – even if that success is perseverance, inner fortitude, or learning from one's mistakes – and it is *that* success which gives us self-worth. Self-esteem is a result of achieving a goal, or at least trying, but not the goal in its self.

'And yet this is where society is headed; entire generations have been brought up to believe in themselves while skipping over the necessary steps that should lead them *to* believe in themselves. There is a lull in effort, in self-determination, in striving towards something of essential value; people think they can buy happiness, they wish for bigger televisions and nicer cars and winning the lottery... they're not wishing for self-fulfilment and good health and an end to third-world poverty. School, college, the professional world, its all a numbers game; and what comes out the other end but a society searching for meaning and happiness and only finding often vain and persistent ways of shallowly achieving it.'

We tottered our way further down the parade until we came to another symbolic building of obsession and ego pandering. I could feel the hairs on the back of my neck stand up; my drunkenness awakened a repulsion in me. A monstrous stone edifice, built on barbarity and conquest in the name of *love* (love!), now more and more becoming a cob-webbed tomb echoing morally objectionable phrases to a class of people who have not yet developed the testicular fortitude to step outside their egocentric cocoon of self-praise, self-worth, and self-proclaimed superiority for the fear of punishment they themselves create.

And isn't this why such a by-gone era of understanding, of creation, of moral behaviour is still able to perpetuate itself: that we are merely bolting our lives down, unconsciously adopting or accepting unquestioned ways of life, stuffing in as fast as we can undigested and impersonal life experiences because the awareness we have of our own existence, our unique and individual life, is so narrow and so superficial that the simple act of *just being* seems to us so boring, that we are itching to fill our time pursuing, very often, quite meaningless and hollow activities in the hope of some future reward. Is it surprising then that such a manner of living leaves us so bare and empty that we have developed an insatiable hunger for an infinite future?[1] An immortality not so much as earned in this life but begged for to come in the next because *this one* is filled with so much self-imposed suffering and boredom?

How is it possible that the lofty height of enlightened man can be bored with *being*? Aha! Well, then deep down we must be destined to become beyond what we are, beyond this shell of monotony and ignorance, *beyond what we know*, if only we bothered to realise this. And to live your life in a constant state of servitude only fulfils the destiny of the few whom are being served: the rulers, the rule makers, the kings and queens, the priests and pastors, the CEOs, the stockholders – these people drive your fate, and for the bent knee then a shameful God your faith.

I walked up the smooth slate stairs to the hugely arched wooden doorway, it was adorned with colossal black iron knockers, and had been left ajar despite the chill of the night – welcoming any of God's straying lambs a warm salvation. I peeked inside; the pastor was giving a sermon to a group of twenty or so; a mix of men and women, mostly middle-aged, mostly bored husbands and wives. A life of piety always leaves one parched for the sweetness of living.

The Church was dimly lit, and the ceiling pitched away into darkness. A few candles burned on the altar under which hung an enormous crucifixion made lively and grotesque from the dancing shadows. *No wonder these places are being abandoned.* I motioned for Harvey to follow me in. I did this on occasion; go to Church to see what took place, what was said that comforted people so, made them feel whole.

The pastor was a tall man in his fifties wearing neat yet casual clothing; a blue sweater over a grey shirt, dark grey trousers, his white collar clearly displayed. As we quietly shuffled along one of pews towards the back, a few people turned and met us with warm smiles (I returned the sentiment), but most listened attentively to the sermon. The pastor did not read from the lectern, instead he stood only a few feet from the devout in the first row, speaking from the Bible with warmth and sincerity, glancing up occasionally while reciting the well-rehearsed words.

'Are these people so short on self-esteem,' I whispered to Harvey, 'so concerned with being made to feel special, so necessary in their life that they need to come to this dreary place and worship something beyond themselves? Worshipping, I can only suppose, what they think they aren't, what they need to be taught – love, generosity, kindness, morals? That they are so compelled to beg and pray for it, and for forgiveness if they have a naughty thought or two?'

We watched them for a few minutes, all nodding together, *amen*-ing together, giggling together. 'You see,' I started, 'there is such a thing called a participation mystique, and the common man is sweetly swayed by it. But it is nothing other than an unconscious identity, an unconscious relationship formed by everyone else present, singing and chanting together.'[2]

'How does it work?' Asked Harvey.

'Well, the group experience takes place on a lower level of consciousness than the individual experience; the inevitability of a large crowd is always a mob mentality. And so, when many people gather together to share one common emotion, the total level of consciousness emerging from the group is below the level of the individual. As the experience continues, one is literally carried along with all the others by this collective wave of identity. One sheep among a thousand! But because this crowd serenades itself with divine blessing and praise, the individual feels great and wonderful, a hero exalted along with the rest of the group, and for doing what exactly? The presence of so many people together, thinking and feeling the same thing, exerts tremendous suggestive force. The one sheep in the flock falls victim to his own suggestibility. They learn to crave the group experience, the group identity, they are eager to return again and again to feel wholly special, to exalt their personality to a higher pedestal unachievable by themselves. And how convenient. This heightened sense of life is achieved only by regressing their unconscious identity, by simplifying their themselves, their individuality, and so the basis for this personal development, this new and exalted rank of being is largely false and unearned.'[3]

'Yes, but,' Harvey began, 'a group can give an individual courage, direction, and even self-respect he may otherwise not achieve on his own. The mob mentality doesn't necessarily have to rule him does it? It can awaken something in him, a self-belief, a confidence.'

'Quite right. Psychiatrists, support groups, family and friends; they all offer similar guidance or advice to self-empowerment. But the Church is different; it requires you to submit, to surrender yourself, and to take in another, dogmatic and generic frame of thinking, a mode of thought applicable to everyone as though must think the same. Sounds rather cultish all of a sudden doesn't it? In any case, it is a dangerous road, to not think critically for oneself, and a road the common man has been conned into following all too easily, for, as I said, it allows something to be added to the individual which he would not otherwise possess. Make no mistake, such unearned gifts may seem fortunate at the time, but since man has a weak habit of taking gifts for granted, there is a risk the gift becoming a loss, or a crutch, and in the long run instead of applying the effort to obtain them himself he demands them as a right.'[4]

'Hmm.'

'Remember Socrates's perhaps most famous statement: 'the unexamined life is not worth living!' Now tell me, which of these little lambs has examined their life, their beliefs, and why they believe them? Show me a man who can be good without God and he is everywhere. Now show me a man who can be bad despite being with God and he is present throughout human history.'

We hadn't realised that, still slightly drunk, our voices had raised and we had inadvertently interrupted the sermon. The pastor stood in the aisle next to the furthest most-back members of his congregation, guarding his flock, and a few pews in front of us.

'My dear boys, is there a question I may help you with?' He said warmly with all the eyes of the parishioners upon us.

A little embarrassed, we blushed and shuffled in our seat. 'Ahem, sorry,' Harvey began, 'no.'

The pastor smiled and went to turn away.

'Actually,' I spoke up, 'I have a question – may I speak candidly?'

'Go ahead,' the pastor smiled again.

'I take it you are reading from the King James Version of the New Testament, father?'

'Of course.'

'Well, if I may, it concerns me, father, as an avid reader of the good book, that this New Testament still includes a book from Paul on how a Christian is to keep and maintain his slaves?'[5]

There was an awkward silence; the pastor not realising that was the end of my question.

'S-slaves, did you say?'

'Yes, father,' I pressed. '*Slaves.*'

'Well,' he cleared his throat, 'let me first say, respectfully, that this is not the time for such a discussion. I am in the company of parishioners who have come to spend their evening in prayer, sermon, and to receive the Lord's blessings. But that said, I shall honour you with a brief answer, if it pleases.'

The congregation bent themselves around eager to heed their pastor's wise and trusting words.

'The first thing that one must do when reading the Bible is separate the myth from the truth, the symbolism from the certainty –'

'And the right from wrong, presumably?' I cut in.

'Well, yes, I suppose that too. But what you must understand -'

'You would concede that much of the moral guidance expressed throughout the Bible has been modernised by society and culture over time, would you not?'

'Well, perhaps to a certain degree, but at its core –'

'But if the Bible is the Christian source for morality, for conducting one's life with good and just behaviour, as inspired by the word of God, how can any aspect of it be incorrect or, dare I say, immoral?'

These questions didn't challenge the pastor so much as they irritated him. 'I, like most Christians, are aware that the Bible has been interpreted and translated from its original form, and within that process some of Jesus's teachings have unfortunately been misinterpreted over time. And so it is up to us, leaders of the church as well as the individual to *see through* what are perhaps literary mistakes and decide for ourselves what our loving God was intending us to hear.'

'But if you are able to decide what of it is morally objectionable, in other words pick and choose the right from wrong, as most modern Christians do, doesn't that imply you already have a moral compass *outside* of the instruction of the Bible? What then, is the Bible teaching us that humanity hasn't been able to establish for itself and of its own insight?'

He started to rally himself, 'Faith. The Holy Spirit. The *true* story of our divine creation,' he said frankly; it was obvious he wanted to continue this no further.

'Please forgive me. I did request to speak candidly, and perhaps I've gone too far.' The pastor forced a smiled. 'But I'm just trying to understand one's religiosity –' two older women scoffed audibly '– in that, if one cannot reconcile the gross hypocrisy found in the Bible, then perhaps the story of Jesus is better understood as a metaphor for one's life rather than a strict and abstinent guideline to follow from what were perhaps many things that never happened in a largely misleading book. Is it possible that Jesus wasn't the embodiment of God, if he existed at all, and was just a man that chartered his life to speaking out and opposing the injustices of the Roman Empire?'

People shifted uncomfortably on their pews, glancing sideways at one another.

'Well, of course I believe that Jesus was *indeed* the embodiment of God. Sacrificing himself was the ultimate display of love for us, his children, his creation.'

'Yes, this is what I've always wondered; why did God have to kill his only son? Why couldn't he have just, say, forgiven us?'

'Because he was showing us that he was willing to die for our sins!'

'And what sins are they? What are sins to someone who has never heard of Jesus? What sins has a newborn baby committed, father, that it deserves to be born with deformity or terminal illness?'

He frowned, unable to hide his deep discomfort for my relentless probing. 'Young man, I cannot explain God's will, but man is far from perfect; he is born with *original* sin. This is why we are but made only in the image of God, and through a life of honest work, servitude, and constant worship do we show Him, Jesus Christ our Lord and Saviour, our love and devotion, so that He will absolve us of our sins, and one day let us into the Kingdom of Heaven where we shall spend eternity in his grace.'

'But, father, for original sin to be true you have to believe that Adam, made from dirt, and Eve, borne of Adam's *rib*, were the first two human beings on Earth, and that Eve is solely responsible for letting 'sin' unto this world? This is one of the myths or symbols you spoke of, no? You surely don't believe that?'

'I assure you I do.' He said confidently.

'Well, I concede that it can be difficult to comprehend the enormous amount of time that it has taken the human species to reach this much celebrated stage of evolution, but it is not impossible. And if it is then there are many, many other places one only has to look to see that humans weren't just magic-tricked into being.'

'Yes, and one of those is a book called *Genesis*.'

'But father, please, we know that ancient Egyptian civilisation predates the Garden of Eden scenario by tens of thousands of years. That ancient African, Chinese, Mayan, and Aztec civilisations (amongst others), and all their monuments and buildings and artefacts, *all* predate Adam and Eve. There's fossil records, carbon dating, gene sequencing; these observations and findings are, well, undeniable. And isn't this the nasty predicament the Christian concept of the world finds for itself when put into this irrefutable historical context; that without Adam and Eve there would be no original sin? That the *fundamental* reason for why a Christian feels the need to, or is supposed to, believe *in* Jesus is inherently flawed? The Bible, this garbled assortment of hypocritical, contradictory, and just plain weird stories evokes within you more reason and logic than what we actually know to be true. That *tens of thousands* of scientists and science facilities around the world, whose grasp and understanding of life and the physical nature of the world, whose knowledge and innovations benefit our lives in innumerable ways every day, would *all* have to have their biology, chemistry, physics, and who knows what else, mixed up, flawed, and wrong. And in its place, it makes more sense to you that God decided to have a revelation in an illiterate dustbowl in the middle of the desert, and bestow upon a bunch of uneducated goat herders divine and infinite wisdom as to the origins of life and the moral code to follow it by?[6] This, as a rational and intelligent, thinking person in the twenty-first century, you find to be more true and compelling?'

The parishioners became irate, the mob mentality in full effect. The pastor, looking as though he was itching to curse at me, spoke through pursed lips, 'I think it would be best if you kindly leave this church, young man.'

'Perhaps only a couple hundred years ago or so,' I carried on, unperturbed by his request, 'when the vast majority of the population were barely educated, *if at all*, hardly literate, you were most likely a peasant, a farmer, or some kind of labourer, smelly and stinking because you bathed once or twice a week, owning the same few pairs of old, musky clothes. No such thing as clean pairs of socks, just a pair of tights full of dead skin, tinea, maybe mould in winter. No underwear either, just your underclothes, the same pair probably and stained in those places that are most embarrassing. Maybe shoes, maybe just muddy feet, but reeking, always reeking. Your only understanding of the world was that it was flat, the sun revolved around us, and we were only a few thousand years old, and if any educated so-and-so whose ideas were so beyond your comprehension that they must of course have been a lunatic, tried to conceive otherwise was branded a heretic and had their tongue pulled out with a hot-poker, their limbs stretched or broken, perhaps disembowelled if the mood was right, or just plain burnt alive in the town square. Yes, of course during such times it's obvious to us how such medieval dogma prevailed. But surely you, father, you living at a time of such scientific and intellectual prosperity, you have at least plumbed the question as to what is the point in persisting in this delusion, irrespective of how comforting it is?'

He was aghast. 'Shut up! That is enough! I will not have you ridicule Christianity in the Lord's house!'

'You think this, a few mild and reasonable objections would offend *Him*?' My tone so casual it only infuriated him further. 'I assure you there is far worse happening in this world as we speak, like rape and murder and innocent little children starving to death? And there are far worse people than me, many of whom are even religious, can you imagine. Oh, I doubt very much He'll be paying much attention to us just now,' I said frankly.

An older woman, her face flushed, stood up with a burst, 'You are wicked, just wicked!' She yelled.

'Well, allow me to read from the Bible if I may,' I said standing, 'let your women keep silence in the churches: for it is not permitted unto them to speak; but they are commanded to be under obedience, for it is a shame for women to speak in the church. One Corinthians fourteen: thirty-four to thirty-five.'[7]

She gawked in disbelief, her mouth agape and quivering.

'Get out!' The pastor erupted. 'Get out! Get out!' He pointed to the entrance; his face red and boiling with fury. *Where is your temperance now?*

The pastor watched us with glassy eyes as we shuffled along the pew and down the aisle. Back outside we burst into drunken laughter.

'You are too much sometimes,' Harvey said with a tear in his eye.

It was all just banter really; indeed they got very upset, and perhaps that was unkind of me, but truth typically causes anger only when one is living a lie. Surely, I did not tell these people anything they have never heard before.

We continued walking in the cold night, this time away from the noise and lights. 'Should I feel ashamed for that?' I asked Harvey, seriously. 'Should I feel ashamed for telling them what is true?'

'*Ahh,* people are free to believe what they wish in

this world,' he said sensitively.

His words hurt me; it took the position that so many of us do, implying that there is no harm in believing in something that is morally absurd or socially destructive.

'That may be true, but you are not free of the consequences that those beliefs hold.' I was upset again all of a sudden. We were silent a moment. "Sometimes people do not want to hear the truth because they do not want their illusions destroyed,[8] Nietzsche said that. Irrespective of that ambush that just took place (it was all comical really), of course there *could be* some divine power, a universal consciousness weaving its way through the quantum web of every-thing, but what it definitely *isn't* is this so obviously contrived piece of unconscionable human imagination ineffectively veiled as divine revelation. Those people in there were Christians, why? Not because of some divine truth, but because of simple geography and childhood indoctrination. If they were born in Israel they'd all probably be Jewish. If they were born in Saudi Arabia they'd be Muslim. In India then Hindu. And yet they can come up with all very sound arguments for why all these other gods are false in their eyes but don't apply them to their own. Absurd!'

'Mmm.'

'No,' I said decidedly, 'I let them off easy for what was my discrepancy but one of a hundred reasonable arguments against the Bible's word, against His word; and yet, how can anything be more reasonable than that – God's word!? And tell me, what modern day believer, imbued with all the moral decency and ethics and understanding forged by reason and logic would stand by their faith if they still burned not one but a hundred heretics a day in the middle of town bearing witness to the screams of agony as the flames licked their flesh and charred their skin? What was God's moral agenda when that was happening? And if it was okay then then why not now? Or what about children beaten and starved, raped and butchered; what God of such foul cruelty deserves worship? Should man *want* to worship?

'And isn't this the problem nowadays; people argue over trifling matters of fact, matters that logically should persuade even the simplest of people but religion is not a matter of fact, far from it. It is emotional, it burrows and toils deep in our subconscious, and this is why logical matters of fact don't dissuade the religious, facts don't matter to them, they don't mean anything otherwise religion would be left alone today and forgotten tomorrow. Anyway, these thoughtful discussions of matter of fact lead us away from a far simple reality of conjecture; that if there were a god, any god for any people, it surely would not permit the brutality and torture of children. Could we not agree on that?'

'Well, I suppose we could,' Harvey agreed.

'And so, if your god *does* permit such atrocious cruelty, irrespective of how supposedly loving elsewhere, how can one turn a blind eye to it? As though, oh well, he does an okay job here and there to make up for it. Is it not logical then to conclude that god is not able to prevent such daily atrocities? And if so then he is not all-powerful, and if he is not all-powerful then why worship a being who is so incapable of maintaining basic justice and equality?

'Surely the only reason religion still functions in modern society at all is because of the tolerance towards the moderate belief it has largely become. A lot of young people call themselves Christian, or whatever else, out of tradition but live their lives without the slightest Biblical following. And yet the notion of a god that created everything just as still festers and bolsters a skewed way of understanding the world.'

'But is it really that bad?'

'Yes, only its effect on society has just become more subtle over time. For certain it was more obvious in the past; the burning of libraries, censorship of philosophers and writers, suppression of all ideas and discoveries that contradicted the notion of God and creation, public torture, the Crusades, and so on, but the intrusion of wilful injustice is still present; no one should have to live under the laws or expectations of another's belief system and yet we do: marriage, sexuality, medical research and procedures, our education, our moral and human rights, they are all negatively impacted. Religion penetrates all of these and either denies or at least encumbers our endeavours and opportunities to progress culturally, socially, humanistically.

'And this is why we cannot remain impartial or apathetic towards something that is reliably and continually destructive, let alone absurd. Religious people take the Bible literally enough to reject what almost all science says about the world, nature, and the cosmos but they don't take it literally enough to feed the poor. Or how about literally enough to not eat pork, shellfish, stone people with tattoos or banish women while they're menstruating. It's palpably absurd. And why give us God's word as a riddle. The riddle is appealing only to the fool for he thinks there is truth and knowledge hidden in it and it is all a pretty little game to get lost in. But really, why would God speak in a riddle, at all?'

We walked on, directionless through the streets, the alcohol wearing off. 'No, a real god wouldn't need constant worship or praise or recognition, it wouldn't need or want great edifices built in its honour, or require crusaders to venture off into the world to murder and pillage innocent people for hundreds of years in order to convert them to his 'benevolent' way of life. If a truly omnipotent god created the world and inspired a book to be written according to his will, why does it reflect only the culture, science, history, technology, and morality of the time in which it was written? And why is god so petty and vengeful, misogynistic and jealous, and torturous?'

'I guess I hadn't really considered the depth to which the Christian mindset penetrates society.'

'Make no mistake, institutionalised religion is a mechanism to impose the will of the powerful on the weak; it always has been. It is every bit social doctrine, cultural delusion, and finally, it is political power warping people's emotions and opinions. And to remain so ignorant is a choice in this age rich in information and knowledge. But you can't tell people this because there is no sensitive way of saying, 'everything you believe is utter nonsense.'

'Society may have needed religion at some point in the past, to make sense of the deeply complex world of nature and man's burning desire to understand not just it but his place in it, a sense of guidance or belonging, but we certainly don't need it now. Today, religion has hijacked man's connection to the world, to nature, and more recently, to the universe. But religion prevents the pious mind from discovering this, from realising this; the religious man cannot accept that we are a product of nature, of evolution, because for him to accept that then the Bible must be so awfully wrong, it must be so obviously contrived by man, *it must be made up*. Those people back there, not because of God's grace, but because of absolute potluck geography live lives far greater than *billions* of other people, but did they ask to be born here, now? Did they ask to be born white? To so-and-so parents in such-and-such country? No, of course not, and yet they attribute this arbitrariness to some non-existent divine blessing.'

My breath plumed as I spoke, the passion with

which I spoke heating my body, 'The fact of the matter is, if you don't want to change how you think then you will not grow. And progress is impossible without change. And the great mockery of the common religious man, his great paradox, listen carefully Harvey, is this: he never *truly* despairs, he never truly dies. Through whatever tragedy befalls him, and through the absolute worst that life offers him, his internal faith and hope fortifies him against any true bearing of his soul, for this personal God is always with him, always protecting, and always preventing anything other than Himself in.[9] And what *is* Him but the well-documented corrupted ideas of the elite and powerful.[10] Remember, Jesus, if he existed at all, was not a Christian. He did not follow a scripture or dogma. He was just a man speaking true to his heart. Nothing more.

'But today, the common religious man tries vigorously to keep hold of himself, of his true nature; he is terrified of his genuineness, of losing himself to his passions, of accepting himself as he is, and so controls and deceives himself into this belief that he must be noble, and moral, and dignified, just as 'God' wants him to be.[11] But this is only a wish, a front, a facade for on the inside he is nature, he is uncontainable, boundless, and above all he is (wonderfully) human, all too human. He has had the wool pulled over him, told that the shadows on the wall are real, and so long as this fear and belief is imposed upon him, he will always choose unhappiness over uncertainty.

'The frightful reality is there are far too many lazy and scared people in the world, Harvey, and conveniently religion offers such an easy method of salvation that it is of course naturally appealing to them in place of the effort and risk of rejecting what you take for granted or for comfort.[12] And religious dogma offers the easy way out for this all too human predicament: that is, that man is self-aware and therefore must be self-controlling, but if he is to control himself then what aspect of himself is doing the controlling? This quandary spooks him, and so it is easier, safer, and devoid of responsibility to give himself over. He says I need to be shown how to be moral, how to be decent, and that way is according himself with God and His divine plan supposedly etched out two-thousand years ago. But if everything is God's plan, if God has intended with his infinite wisdom for destiny to unfold for each and every one of us a certain way, well then, there is no such thing as morality, or even responsibility. For how can I be responsible for my actions, my transgressions if it was God that intended them to happen just so, willed me to do them? And then for what use is praying? Is this not laughable, Harvey?'

'Okay, but what about those that say there isn't a preordained plan for us, and that God judges people on the right and wrong of their actions?'

'Well, I would say that within the religious worldview there is very much an anxiety to be right, a moral urgency to act appropriately, to be noble and dignified, and religion will claim it offers the way to that: God.[13] God is the apparent right from wrong, the good against evil, the good in everything that permeates throughout the world, and so to be immoral or to be in the wrong is to be against God, to shame God, and to be cast out not just from society (where the religious worldview unconsciously dominates), but also from existence itself. To be in the wrong – any wrong, trivial or serious, for who can say what God's taste is, or hasn't wronged at some time in their life let alone this month or this week? Today even? – therefore arouses a deep sense of guilt and anxiety, to be punished with some degree of damnation. And this is of course utterly disproportionate to the crime. And this deep anguish and guilt is so insupportable that when questioned, when considered reasonably, eventually issues the very rejection of God and his laws.[14] Is there any surprise that in developed nations religiosity is spectacularly declining? That because we *know* there is no old bearded man sitting above the clouds, we do not fear Him, we no longer seek forgiveness from some wrathful God lurking above, watching our every move, listening to our every thought.

'And yet a conflict of ideologies still remains because religion, as a social mechanism for control, is still being thrust upon us, even in its archaic form. The common religious person is exhausted, frustrated in his efforts to live accordingly to self-contradictory goals, and so his unique function, whatever that may be, is lost. And since there is nothing truly inspiring achieved in his life, other than being a humble servant, his true reason for living is never achieved.[15] He is just lead down a path to live mindlessly and work monotonously for some future reward, some kind of salvation, some material version of Heaven on Earth, and if not for him, then for his children. And so this inherently creates a type of human being that fails to really live in the present, that fails to create beyond themselves.

'The stark reality is this: the psychological development, or rites of passage, in which mythology and religious symbolism guided the spiritual experience of previous generations, simply no longer applies today (whether religious or not) because these inherited beliefs fail to represent the real problems of contemporary life. Instead, we are now struggling to face these dangers alone in a world where the ideological compass has shifted tremendously, and our problem as enlightened individuals is that we have rationalised all the gods and devils out of existence.[16]

'Free from bondage, from unnecessary tradition, the spell of the past has lifted, and the web of myth fallen away. In the fateful words of Nietzsche's *Zarathustra*, indeed dead are all the gods,[17] and now like a butterfly from its cocoon, modern man has emerged from ancient ignorance. No longer is there a hiding place for gods to sit their thrones, but there is also no society as the gods once supported. Society is now largely an economic and political identity, and has outgrown its call to pass on trifling religious content. Only do the sweet dream-bound mythologies remain in remote and isolated areas, and unexploited by man's lust for power and control are they able to preserve their uncorrupted spiritual connection to the Earth. But within the developed society, where a phony and unanimous identity is formed, we see in full decay every last vestige of ritual, morality, and art from our ancient past.[18] For good and for bad.

'The problem set before mankind today, unlike his ancestors that benefited and orientated himself with the great mythologies of the past, is this: millennia ago, all meaning and purpose of life were contained within the group whole, in countless and anonymous forms, and none in the unique, self-expressive individual; today, no meaning is in the group, society is merely a stage, all meaning is within the individual, but now the meaning is absolutely unconscious.[19] The achievements of science and technology are not without cost, and our rationalistic and pragmatic view of reality only compounds our clouded disconnection to the natural world. It is with much poignancy that I say one does not know towards what one moves; one does not know by what one is propelled.'[20]

As it happened, during this lengthy and exhausting conversation in which I poured out every last drop of feeling, every last thought on the matter (I had nothing left, nothing at all), we had managed to walk all the way back to my building. We sat on the rooftop, as we customarily did, and watched in silence the blurry lights of the city melt into the landscape far beyond.

Somewhere far off, faintly, car horns blew, shouts rang, somewhere closer laughter; in between everything the sound of sirens hung in the still air. Remnants of these sounds echoed their way up between the buildings draped in the darkness of the night; neglected and overborne stars twinkled through the patchwork of clouds that hid all but a sliver of the moon. Our moods were reflective, yet not sombre; our deep, laborious breaths our only conversation. A sublime moment amongst the chaos.

Finally, Harvey broke the silence, 'What now, Will?'

I contemplated my answer for several moments. 'What I have noticed, tonight, just now, is a sudden and profound relaxation. I feel a kind of utter abandonment for any purpose, any goal. I am reminded of an old saying, I don't know from where, perhaps a dream: when the purpose has been used to achieve purposelessness, the thing has been grasped. The past few nights have had an overpowering effect on me. I feel all of a sudden endowed with all the time in the world, and my journey is only just begun. I feel free to look around, to discover what is true, as if I were living in eternity.'

I suddenly laughed to myself, realising that this is why I find so comical the endless busying and fussing actions of the common man, that by giving himself goals which are always in the future, in the tomorrow that never comes, he is missing exactly what it means to be alive.[21]

'I understand why it is the common man grieves me so; he has become so self-conscious that he shuns away from his very own consciousness. He runs from his inner turmoil, his inner conflict of misunderstanding who and why he is. This is why he is so petty and judges. He seeks value and validation and identity in the trivial and always changing external world. It is no surprise then that he lacks so much substance, so much unique expression, so much wonder not just in the world around him but of himself. He finds nothing fascinating in what it is to be truly human; it has never astonished him because he is looking in all the wrong places.' I was dizzy with sudden excitement.

'You're right; so few people have an understanding of themselves,' Harvey added distantly.

'Yes! Understanding, or better yet, self-awareness.' Something ignited within me. 'It is *self-awareness* that makes the human experience resonant, evocative, and glorious. Without it life is shallow, flat, devoid of the sublime depth and volume one feels when their being is in accordance with destiny. *Amor fati.*'[22]

'*Amor fati*?'

'Oh yes! It is that sweet nihilist,[23] Nietzsche: 'I want to learn more and more to see as beautiful what is necessary in things; then I shall be one of those who make things beautiful. *Amor fati*: let that be my love henceforth! I do not want to wage war against what is ugly. I do not want to accuse; I do not even want to accuse those who accuse. Looking away shall be my only negation.'[24] What a beautiful thought! It is all beginning to make such sense now, Harvey. Suffering and loss are just as necessary to the soul as joy and pleasure. We mustn't fight it.' I immediately thought back to the church just now, the parishioners; so they might be fools, but who am I to tell them so. If they feel they need it, as if there was no other choice, then, perhaps, they should have it.

'How? How does one learn to love their fate, no matter what?'

'Acceptance, Harvey, of all that there is and all that we've become. Oh, and rejection too, rejection of everything that is false in us. We must have the courage to cast off what we cannot swallow, what is no good for the human soul. Only when we are willing to let go of everything can we allow a deeper truth to come forth and penetrate us. And within this doing there will be a time of absolute fear – I feel it now, Harvey (yet fear of absolutely nothing). And loneliness and emptiness – I feel that too, but I will not, cannot run from it. Like a journey through the wilderness which no one else can make for us, which no one else can spare us. But this, this is the very life-journey that people are unwilling to take; and in return they will continue to receive all that they already know.'

'Is that where you feel you are? At the edge of that, that wilderness?'

I starred longingly towards the soft haze of light emanating from the city; I felt weightless and airy, as though drifting up into the atmosphere to meet some new horizon that I knew was there, that I knew awaited me. 'Yes, Harvey, I think so.' I said thoughtfully.

As I went to sleep that night, I realised, perhaps fully for the first time, that to be shattered, to be born anew within this lifetime (perhaps again and again), we mustn't look for verbal answers. Rather, if metaphysical wonder is what we wish to unfold within us, then it will come in the form of an experience, a vision, a stunning revelation that will explain with such clarity and truthfulness, why everything is so,[25] and why we are living one of our thousand lives.

PART II

TWELVE
SAD AND GLIMMERING

THE FOLLOWING DAY, Amy called and asked to see me. I told her I had taken the day off and arranged to meet her after she finished work. She sounded sad, hurt by the conflict from the previous night; less from anything that happened to be said, and more from the harsh truth of our ongoing disconnection that had continued to dampen our once besotted and love-struck relationship.

I sat with my curtains drawn; the late afternoon sky was dark and depressed, filled with heavy rain clouds. Peaking between the blinds I looked nonchalantly out over the drizzly concrete landscape and lost myself in thought. It was so different during the day, the city (especially from this lofty vantage), so boring and lifeless. I pictured people hurrying their lives in such a mad inconsiderate rush; their day filled with appointments and deadlines and agendas and meetings and quotas. And what did it matter? What was it all achieving? Just the slightest turn of a giant rusted cog; as though the entire economic world was a colossal wristwatch and each day the collective effort of every single human being across the country made the hands heave one revolution of its corroded gears. I felt detached, distant; but I seemed to no longer care.

My thoughts drifted to Amy. She was someone I could marry; perhaps should marry. But I realised that made her exactly why I didn't want to. I now knew it meant the end; the end of drifting, of losing myself because I'd no longer be lost. I'd be someone's, fixed, and settled, ready to address the more sensible things in life: dinner parties and home renovations, family do's and of course little bundles of joy; check each one off the list like they're all inevitabilities. Because for the common man they are – they're milestones, statuses even and yet so far from actually living. And so, the belt of predictability whips my soul once again, lashing at my spirit, my will to exist in every which way but one.

No, I couldn't. I still had so much to learn in life; about myself, about everything. It was then I was filled with guilt and sadness; I felt horribly selfish, mean even, to have dragged her through my mess of living, to have wasted her time, to have tempted her heart into loving me, caring for me, this shell, this ghost... this wolf in a man's skin. I felt a little sick. But how was I to know; how was I to know that it would unfold this way? That I would unfold this way? I did love her. I probably still do. She is sweet and gentle and smart; and only wants to love.

We met in the city near her work; her architecture firm was situated in quite a trendy part of town and was surrounded by cafes, restaurants, fashion stores, and so on. As twilight gently descended over the sky, several of the cafes and restaurants had patrons already indulging in after work drinks and early dinners; and despite the cool autumn air, many people dined alfresco under the glow of warm heaters; their wine glasses shimmering, their mood jovial.

We hugged awkwardly and sat down.

'So.' I said after a moment.

'So?'

'How was work?' I asked, fumbling to start the conversation.

'Fine. The usual; the project I'm on has been delayed.'

'Oh,' I said, trying to sound sympathetic.

'How come you took the day off work?'

'I wasn't feeling well. It's nothing.'

'Okay. That's good.' She chewed her lip and her eyes fidgeted.

'Look, Amy…' I apologised for upsetting her, for not appreciating her misunderstanding; for, in the end, any or all of her misunderstanding firstly began with me. This was the right of it; she could be in a number of different places right now, and no doubt all of them far better than the wretched mess I offered her, this I knew. Would she be better off? Would she be happier, now or later? Would she just become another Ms Anderson from HR in fifteen or twenty years? I didn't know, but nor should I be the one to hold her back if that was her fate… her *amor fati*.

We were quiet again.

No, in the end, Amy was innocent. What did I have to offer except my own delirious confusions? Perhaps not innocent of being all too common, all too material; no, she was guilty of that, like most, despite my efforts to wring it out of her. But such is the coercive power of this culture and its superficial ideals; inescapable and inexorable are the rules to follow, the job to get, the money to earn, the 'hobbies' to enjoy, and, ultimately, the things to think, and the feelings to feel. This is civil obedience in all its splendour; to obey instead of question, to follow instead of find; and so it is the same for the soldier sent to war, the parishioner threatened of hell, or the common man fearful of not succeeding at life, a life he's forced to live. They are all one and the same.

Then we got started.

'I don't know what's going on with us, Will. You've been so different over these past few months, and then the last few days...' She let her comment trail off. She collected her thoughts and continued, 'I want us to be together but I need to know that it's going to be something more, that it's moving forward, that there is a point to all this.' She was reaching out, hoping, willing me to say the words that would save us, save her.

But they didn't come. And all of a sudden, sitting across from one another, it all became so clear: she was only ever fascinated by me, intrigued, not by what I awakened in her. She loved me deeply, of that I had no doubt, but what *me*? Was she just waiting for me to change, to come around and realise the pressing matters of the bourgeois life I should concede into caring about? No, that wasn't me, and neither I am to change in that way, to reduce myself. As the beast said, 'I will forfeit many things lovely and pretty and sweet in this world,' and here indeed was one of them.

She didn't see all of me, and she just showed it: 'I need to know that there is a point to all this,' and what if there wasn't? Or what if this – whatever we were or had become, *was* the point, then what? Isn't she missing it then? And isn't it such a human quality, such a hedonistic flaw, to regard the things that do not go to plan as 'bad,' as though there was nothing one got out of the choice they made, out of the suffering? When, in all reality, our lives are filled with a multitude of endings and beginnings, interludes, and it is only our desire to control and predict our lives that we see certain experiences in a certain light, when in fact, they are all just experiences, as equal and as fair as each other.

I didn't answer her question. Her delicate face was drawn, her brown eyes dark and full of watery sadness; *her heart aches.*

'Do you believe in true love?' She asked.

'I believe there is someone for everyone, for a time.'

'For a time?'

'Maybe for their whole lives; but maybe not.'

'Do you think love is what makes it work? What keeps people together?'

I considered her question for a moment, 'I think

love may be there at the beginning and not at the end, or not at the beginning but there at the end; but I think its compatibility, something like that, that makes it work.'

'Do you think we are... compatible?'

Perhaps not so long ago I would have answered with something comforting, even if I wasn't sure it to be true; but not now, we were too far gone. 'Not anymore.' That was the truth.

She swallowed hard. 'Were we ever?'

It was a reflective question, a question for the past, a question clutching for something that would make her feel good now and not so hopeless. A question typical when an end is near and you want to make sense of why, despite your best efforts, it hasn't worked out. 'I'm not sure,' I replied, perhaps too uncaringly.

'I guess it doesn't really matter, does it?' She said despondently; she was right. 'But we were so good together. What happened?'

'I suppose, just because something is good doesn't mean it won't end,' I said quietly. It's not that I believe nothing 'lasts forever,' it's that nothing *should* last forever. I thought about the last few days of my life, the swirling of something queer and cosmic at play, and I realised, distractedly, the world is anew, every day, and it is only our inability to see this that makes it such a struggle.

'Then why – why even start, Will? Why even love me, and let me love you if you felt this way?' She was upset, angry, and perhaps rightfully so. Tears welled in her eyes.

'I don't know,' I said hotly, more than I meant to. 'I didn't mean for this, I didn't mean to feel the way I do about life, about what I want to do.'

'What *do* you want to do?' She was tired of my confusion, my shiftlessness, my indirection; and who could blame her. She was patient of the indecision I showed towards career, towards settling down, but she had a limit, like all sensible people, a time frame for when reality, her reality, had to take over.

'I want to go places, see things I've never seen before, feel things I've never felt,' I said passionately. 'I don't know what I want but I know I don't want life to pass me by; I don't want to die before I even get to start, leave it too late, not know who I am or what I was capable of. Maybe I don't want to do the same thing every day for the next thirty years, wake up in the same city, see the same people.' I realised I was steaming and softened my tone, 'Maybe we're still finding out who we are... and maybe we're becoming different people... growing apart.'

We were quiet a moment before I continued, 'I feel like there is so much more in me that's undiscovered, that's aching to burst out, waiting, wanting to become something else, something more... but I don't know how long it's going to take to find it. And maybe you're right, maybe it's wrong of me to expect you to wait around for that to happen.' I didn't really feel that way but I thought it was good to give her a more real reason.

Amy didn't speak, but she was no longer confused. She understood too well that I yearned for something beyond this menial world of things; beyond what she could offer me.

'I'm sorry, Amy...' I said softly.

She let a tear slowly trace down her cheek; it hung on the side of her face, sad and glimmering. For some strange reason she looked as beautiful as the night I met her; delicate, beautiful, fragile. I wanted to hold her now, as I did that night, and isn't this the pain of letting go, the desire to still hold on.

We sat in a painful, sorry silence; neither of us willing to speak or move first, both aware that there was nothing more to be said. What made it worse was that this was not a bitter ending, it was not a relationship torn apart by turmoil or by cowardly or inappropriate actions. It was but a sad parting of ways, a journey that the two of us could no longer continue on together. Although I have only described our growing differences that have come about recently, the truth is this was quite a disappointing and upsetting end; Amy had loved me very deeply, perhaps in a way that I have misunderstood and will one day regret. But I cannot conceal the sorrow I have for the common man or my reluctance to become him; and there is too much in him that she needs me to be.

Amy began to wipe the tears from her eyes, her mascara smudging on her pale cheeks. She stood up, 'No, I'm sorry. I'm sorry I loved you so much and that I made your life so damn miserable, kept you from being whatever it is you want to be.' She made to leave but turned back for one last word.

'Fuck you, Will.'

THIRTEEN
LET ME TAKE YOU SOMEWHERE

I LEFT THE CAFE AND STARTED FOR HOME. Head down I walked with pace, eager to get back to my apartment, to breathe, to collapse on my bed and let the madness of the past day and night settle into something I could make sense of. I was oblivious to passers-by, unmindful of the richness of my surroundings: the crisp air beginning to fog with my breath, the purple haze that hung at one end of the night sky, the shifting traffic, the joggers in the park, the empty courts, the soul-man belting his sax with sweet tones. I felt sadness in my eyes but at least the knotted guilt that gripped my gut seemed to be finally letting go. At least for now, before both Amy and I lay the first raw moments of our next interludes of this infinite jest. That was something. Amy would be happy again in a few weeks or months, maybe happier than anything I was able to offer her. As for me, all that stood before me now was this dark and lonely journey into the wilderness that I knew was approaching.

In the street a manhole steamed and swirled with magical liveliness, the subway rumbled past below like some giant subterranean beast; time had frozen in the still, dark night and in that moment of nonsense I felt endowed with all the time in the world, free to look around, to discover what is true, as if I were suddenly living in eternity. And despite the sorrow I felt for likely seeing Amy for the last time, I found myself reflecting on my conversation with Harvey; that sudden relaxation and abandonment for any purpose, any goal, came to me now as it did last night on the rooftop. An airy feeling of liberation pulled me up from my slumped shoulders, but it was not without cost, not without sacrifice, and I knew that. I laughed bitterly to myself and began to wander aimlessly through the city; not lost or disorientated, but with jovial carelessness. My mind was abuzz and my body tingled; on the one hand I felt the great vacuum of space that Amy once filled; her sweet touch, her care, her concern. Not everyone is loved, and perhaps I should have taken her affection more sincerely. But I couldn't, not out of choice but for this voyage that I am yet to embark on, and yet where is my vessel? Where is my sea to cross or my valley to descend? Was the beast in the dark just a dream? Was the chaos of these recent days just a cruel ruse? For in this other hand do I hold all that there ever is; the proverbial now. And I am alive, yes I am alive and that was real.

Lost in these thoughts I had strayed towards a part of downtown occupied by a couple of university campuses: campuses for architecture and design, performance and visual arts. Their buildings were colourful, irregular and oddly shaped; some faces were curved, some domed, while others had facades of reflective glass, capturing the melting lights of the city within its mirrored waters. These buildings, art in themselves, stood out noticeably amongst the square brick and concrete office blocks of plain colour and shape that surrounded them. Young students walked in small groups holding their large sketch-books, talking loudly, some laughing, their young optimistic lives brimming with joy as they finished a night of futile study; study that will likely lead to nothing for the most of them. Artists, drawers, poets, dancers, the world of consumerism struggles to have need of you; your faculties are getting smaller and smaller, so yes, maybe laugh now, while you can, while you are able to you. *Enjoy it while it lasts*, I thought warmly.

I began to walk through the narrow lanes and walkways of the campus, drawn in by the vibrancy, the energy contained within the walls, the creativity of thoughts and ideas so lacking elsewhere in the common man's concrete playground. I turned down a dark lane that to my surprise was considerably occupied; there were many people who seemed to be congregating outside of an entrance that was well-lit from the inside. People smoked cigarettes and gossiped loudly, people were coming and going, and everyone was dressed rather fashionably. As I moved closer to the entrance I could see that it was an art exhibition of some sort.

'Quickly, quickly!' An accented voice said, as a hand pulled me from my side. 'Just stand close. Please,' she added.

'What –' I began before getting cut off.

'A little closer. Shh.'

We stood somewhat hidden in the recess of the building next to the busy gallery. She stood too close for me to see her clearly; her head at my neck, her hands holding my coat, pulling us together almost intimately. She smelled of laurel and lemon that blended with a

towards one of the paintings. I stood beside her and studied her for the first time since our strange introduction outside. She had long, straight sandy blonde hair that she wore up in a loose, almost messy ponytail; she had striking grey-blue eyes, a straight nose, soft full lips, and light brown freckles on her cheeks.

'Finished looking,' she said without turning.

'I'm sorry, I didn't mean to.'

'Yes you did. But beauty should be enjoyed.' She turned to face me. 'Do you find me beautiful?' Isabelle said without smiling, her eyes tense and unblinking, as though waiting for a photographer to capture her portrait.

Her boldness caught me off-guard, her matter-of-factness; a trait rarely found in the common man so caught up in his false niceties and hollow attempts at being coy. It wasn't just how she was speaking; it was her demeanour, her manner, the way she tilted her head, the slope of her shoulders; she was especially self-assured, or so it appeared. I savoured her stare and waited a moment before replying. 'Yes,' I said flatly.

'*Bon*. A simple question deserves a simple answer. And what about this?' She nodded towards the small painting before us.

'What about it?'

'Do you find *it* beautiful?' Almost annoyed that I hadn't kept up with the meaning of her question.

It was contemporary art, *conceptual* art; it was a painting that cared more about its meaning then what it looked like and yet, its meaning was entirely lost on me. 'No,' I said thoughtfully.

'Mmm. *Bon.*' She walked to the next painting, making sure to stand directly in front of it. I followed her, swept up in her aroma, her attitude, her accent.

She tilted her head and studied the painting for a brief moment. 'And this?'

'No.'

'Why?'

'Because conceptual art has substituted skill for meaning.'

'Mmm. Go on.'

'Well, it no longer conjures up a beautiful (or ugly) surreal world of its own for the observer to step into; its imagination only goes so far as its idea but its idea is merely a statement about the world, not of some surreal and imaginary place envisioned by the artist. Art has become science or philosophy, making statements, deconstructing, reducing, but this is not what art is meant to be.'

'Mmm, *très bon*.' Isabelle turned and faced me inquisitively. 'There is much to you, isn't there?'

'Just as much as there is in all of us.'

'Oh, *conneries!*' She scoffed. 'Bullshit. Lies. A most many people are boors and clods, and too *stupide* to realise it.' She crossed her arms and took a step towards me; her grey-blue eyes searching. I could smell her sweet perfume, her breath; the look she gave captured me. She continued, 'Your eyes are still in the past, *monsieur*, and I feel like discussing culture tonight, so out with it?'

I parted my mouth but no words came. I was too taken aback, too confused, too spellbound. She was so forthright and frank, a manner that I was not accustomed to. I felt awkward and embarrassed and even a little vulnerable that she could see right through me, see my sadness, my wretched lack for living. And of course, *who was she?* Our sudden meeting only a moment ago was certainly absurd, but so absurd it only carried me along.

'Listen to me, a man's heart is only ever saddened by a woman; otherwise he is only ever angered by what bothers him, no? Tell me, who has broken this handsome boy's poor heart.' She spoke candidly and it would have been easy to mistake her uncomplicatedness for condescension or perhaps mockery, but it was neither of these I realised; she had an irresistible air of abandonment and a sensuous nature that I immediately found both threatening and beautiful.

And so it suddenly dawned on me, that lofty pinnacle of personal desertion and profound relaxation that my life had now seemingly come to, the rejection of pretence and predictability and expectation, the forgoing of menial gratification in the hopes of savouring something sweeter in this lifetime, something subtle, sublime, transcendent; it was all before me, yet still unknown, ungraspable, and yet moments away, perhaps happening now, a stunning interlude beginning, here, under these bright lights with the nakedness of my soul exposed to this stranger, this inquisitor, this splendorous *deus ex machina*. Had all the drama and personal turmoil of the last few days (months, years) happened so such a moment, such a person could be met? An experience not otherwise to be had if not all the experiences were lived prior to it?

'Yes,' I began, 'there is a woman, *was* a woman, gone. Just now, tonight. It needed to end, and sadness is only natural.'

'Why did it need to end?'

I thought for a moment, for my pain was beyond Amy, as sad as I was that she was now gone from my life, but no, my pain was something deeper. 'Because I have lost my faith in humanity, Isabelle.' She didn't seem surprised by this response. I continued anyway, 'I have lost my desire to be a part of this trivial world of men; its lack of substance; its lack of culture. We have lost ourselves, missing is our true sense of self, and in its stead we think identity is something that can be cheaply constructed, but from what I ask you? In recent decades irony has saturated everything that has attempted to be meaningful, and our default posture has become the fruitless questioning and self-deconstructing of all beliefs and narratives.'

I was tired; I felt as though that for the last few days all I had been doing was explaining myself, revealing myself, and yet to what avail? I looked around at all the hopeless conceptual art, and all the people gobbling down its hollowness without an inclination to consider beyond their glib critique of motives, intent, or meaning why it doesn't evoke something profound within them. Can't they see that this is no longer an acceptable response to an idea or question, that this is only the response made by a culture where culture has been lost, that no longer has any intrinsic value to orient itself? I continued bleakly, 'Culture is crumbling; we produce nothing comparable to the great Oriental carpets, Persian glass, tiles, or books, Arabian leatherwork, Spanish marquetry, Hindu textiles, Chinese porcelain and embroidery, Japanese lacquer and brocade, French tapestries,[3] Shakespearean tragedies, or the aristocratic paintings of the Renaissance. Even for the person who wants to become educated or a professional or a businessman, life's well-worn paths walked by older generations are no longer reliable to us, or even exist, and so where does the youth of today – the people of tomorrow – turn to for inspiration, for purpose, for truth, for spiritual happiness, for artistic expression, for anything of essential value? We are lost, drowning, and worst of all we are unconscious to it.' I looked around the gallery in discontent. 'No, deep down we are longing for something more authentic, more genuine, more sincere; this is what is to come next but from where I do not know.'

She stared at me, reading me, deciding something; her face was gentle, deep in consideration, beautiful in the white light. Then, quickly looking around the gallery, she grabbed my hand, 'Come, let us leave these boors and clods to themselves,' she said leading us to the exit. Once we were outside in the laneway Isabelle continued, almost rushing, leading us away from the people gathered at the gallery entrance. We eventually slowed our pace; the autumn air was chilly and Isabelle threaded her arm through mine, huddling me as we walked.

'I'm sorry I did that just now but I needed to leave that place. There was nothing in there for us but gloom and grief, wouldn't you agree?' She left no opening for a response. 'Anyway, I wanted to talk about culture tonight and when I asked you what has broken your heart you told me it was culture! *Ironie du destin*, no?' She said astonished.

We stopped walking; Isabelle turned me so that we were facing each other. 'So, you see, that is why I had to rush out of there; of all the possibilities that this night offered, *this* is the one fate decided to bring on.' She had lost her frankness, her detached indifference, and in its place sparked something that spoke with excitement and wonder. We stood in cold silence, our eyes fixed to each other's; and yet a warmth overcame me, a stirring of something deep and unspeakable. And despite Isabelle's attractiveness, the energy that surrounded us was not one of romance or tenderness, but had the undertones of something quite serendipitous, an allurement of forces not rightly understood.

'Let me take you somewhere?'

'Where?'

'Does it matter, *monsieur*? Everywhere is somewhere.'

'No, I suppose it doesn't.'

'I promise it will be somewhere beautiful.'

And so we went, under the shimmering vigilance of countless neglected stars, overborne and beyond measure, wandering through the cold darkness of our heartfelt destitution for this world, but not in silence, for Isabelle questioned my deep misanthropic sentiments ceaselessly on our journey; her sweet, delicate accent only augmented further the beautiful strangeness of this fateful night.

We boarded an overland train headed for some distant, forgotten suburbs; it was old and badly maintained but still rolled on, albeit much slower than the uptown subways. The advertisements pasted to the walls were mostly out of date, and so too was the graffiti. The stuffing in the brown corduroy seats pushed its way out where the cushion was torn or split, and a broken window with a shard missing let in a cold draught. There were only four people in our cart; an old woman in a grey fur coat clutched her groceries as she sat by herself; a teenage boy in a ragged tracksuit stared distantly at the basketball he held in his hands while (presumably) his younger brother of seven or eight slumped against his arm sleeping; and a middle-aged Mediterranean looking man with a bushy moustache wearing a sad and faded cabbie flat-cap sat across from us reading yesterday's newspaper.

I had begun describing why I thought we had reached such a dreadful understanding of ourselves, 'Perhaps it was the failed dreams of what the Enlightenment period hoped it would bestow upon mankind; by that I mean centralising government, abolishing serfdom, giving people freedom and greater opportunity to be happy and progress in society, and you'd have to say for the most part this worked.'

'So what didn't?'

'Well, in order to achieve all these things, society had to pursue and rely on reason and logic, we chose to draw conclusions from what was observable in nature, what was predictable and measurable and reliable. And with this great movement towards natural science, towards philosophy of morals and ethics, and the desire to have practical and reasoned explanations for things that happened, enlightened society inevitably questioned and eventually began denouncing attitudes or practices that resulted in human injustice or oppression, especially that which was the result of religious dogma. And with that the realisation that we should no longer believe in the otherworldly values offered by religious faith. All gods were indeed now dead in the sense that it was surely time we moved on from a value system predicated on religious superstitions that are handed down to us by a select group of individuals who have no greater connection with God than you or I or a goldfish, and whose moral arguments are wildly contradictory and permit that which is unbelievable, unthinkable, and inexcusable. Instead of liberating us to loftier heights, man, weak in the face of uncertainty, chose not to let go of his superstitious, hedonistic, and vain conception of the world.'

'Mmm.'

'Then, what else have we? Well, on came the industrial revolution, capitalism, the dramatic advancements of science and technology throughout the twentieth-century combined with a rationalistic and pragmatic default view of the world, and there you have it, we have inevitably threatened with total annihilation man's greater spiritual understanding of himself, his place, and his purpose. He has become a robotic slave with a heart that aches. Can we blame him for kissing the feet of a dead god? He thinks no better of himself in this conflicted world where progress is suppressed by the ignorant and fearful.

'I guess in this sense,' I continued, 'there is little surprise that art (as imitating life) now suffers within this interlude of bleak deconstructed conceptual expression for what is it expressing but heavily reduced statements about a world that we have all but extinguished any meaning from. If we use literature as our historical thread, we can see the deep-psychological novels of nineteenth-century Russia (see: Dostoyevsky, Turgenev, Gogol, Chekhov, Tolstoy) that arose from an atmosphere of real nihilism and political upheaval eventually have its optimistic and humanistic view of the world crushed by war, revolution, and poverty. Modern literature shifted to a focus on existentialism but stripped it bare exposing the simple futility and absurdity of man; the potential meaninglessness of our existence seemed only to spur on the common man's blind devotion to old superstitions rather than drive him forward and up beyond our current dimension. And now the artistic world suffers a lack of vision and imagination. And this is in the finer fields of intellectuality and creativity; within the common man's political and social forum there is a different future potentially unfolding, a new wave of censorship and stubbornness to a progressive world, and a return to religious fundamentalism as he claws desperately for some kind of identity regardless of how hollow or constructed for him it is.'

We got off the train after a short trip; the air was colder and the stars slightly brighter. There was less noise on the streets here too; people were either sleeping or working I guessed, the price for revelry a price too high. Outside of the station we walked towards a large park (perhaps more a botanical gardens) that had its gates closed and locked; I knew this place by name but had never come here. Isabelle led us to a bench that sat below a tree whose branches reached across the wall. We stood on the bench and used the branch to help carry us over. It was obvious from Isabelle's swiftness that she had done this many times before. The park was unstirred, eerily quiet, and filled with shadows; and unlike any public parkland in the city that would have lamps illuminating its pathways, this venue had closed its doors for the night and had given itself over to the hallowed stillness such that a stunning wilderness bestows.

'Isn't it beautiful?' Isabelle whispered, inhaling the silence.

We walked slowly from the underbrush by the wall and out into the open gardens. Although it was dark and all I could see were shades of bluey-black, I soon noticed the expanse of the park; manicured paths and flower gardens trailed off in all directions, I could make out a large gazebo off to one side, and dense tree-lined walkways descended into darkness to the either side of us.

'This way,' Isabelle said walking with her returned pace despite the lack of visibility. She said as we walked, 'Where were you? Oh yes, man has lost his way. Please, go on.'

'Well,' I started, 'this is neither the beginning nor the end of the problem, only the thick of it. I fear the current generation has not had the appropriate moral formation for a return to the authentic. For the same reason it is difficult for the compulsive activist to see that mere effort and technique will not solve the vast social and economic problems afflicting the world. The startling truth is that our best efforts will only further destroy rather than help if made in the present spirit of man.'

'How do you mean?'

'I mean we have nothing to give. If our own riches and our own way of life are not enjoyed here, they will not be enjoyed anywhere else. Money is not prosperity, peace can only be made by those who are peaceful, and love shown only by those who are loving. If guilt, fear, or hollowness of heart is what forces peoples or governments to help, then their efforts will not succeed; that is not how love and compassion and empathy work. Our current appetite for living will always come at the cost of some other forgotten, trodden on people. And the same can be said of ourselves, the individual; any valid plans for the future cannot be made by those who have no capacity for living now.[4] Do you see?'

Isabelle listened intently, understanding, but made few responses.

I went on, 'If our identity is cheaply constructed, artificial, and above all else shallow, if this is our moral foundation we might want to fight it but we do not have the resources to come up with any constructive solution, we simply have not developed the necessary virtues. Is there any surprise that we are drowning in mediocrity?

We have nothing else around us to inspire us.'

Up until then I spoke with curious excitement despite the melancholy of my words, but I suddenly fell quiet and stared longingly out into the darkness. I continued, though distantly, 'Sheer force power and sheer will has overtaken us; we've lost the touch, even the vision of what is grand, beautiful, sublime, mystical. Our dependence on the beautiful sciences has inadvertently reduced everything down to mechanical and quantifiable parts; we have choked out all of the transcendence and we need it back, only we do not know how.' My voice was soft and defeated.

It was then I noticed the gentle sound of wood lightly banging against itself, like a wind-chime but the pieces much larger and the knocking much deeper. Within a few feet we were suddenly at the edge of a large lake; the moonlight made the water look as though it was black ink rippling in the breeze. There were about ten or twelve little wooden paddleboats all tied up.

'I hope you know how to row, *monsieur*,' Isabelle said as she begun to untie one from its moorings.

'Where are we going?' I asked curiously.

'There,' she pointed, 'to the beautiful place I promised.'

What Isabelle pointed to was a large grassy island in the middle of the lake, perhaps three-hundred feet away, and on it stood what looked like a very old single-story manse adjoined to an equal size glasshouse. 'Why there?' I asked.

'Because you ask too many questions,' Isabelle said with a smirk as she hopped down into the small boat. 'Come on.'

I stepped down carefully into the paddleboat; I sat with my back to the bow and faced Isabelle who pushed us away from the edge. I took hold of the oars, dipped them gently into the black ink and slowly started to row. After a few strokes I got the handle of how to do it, and so quietly across the lake we went, the water lapping against the side of our vessel, cloaked in darkness and guided by sweet fate. Isabelle folded her arms and held her cardigan tight around her as the wind pulled bits of her loose blonde hair across her face; she stared at me strangely and without hesitation. I met her eyes only occasionally but felt too overwhelmed to hold my glance. I felt flushed and a little foolish; I had revealed so much about myself and yet she had revealed so little.

We were about halfway (as far as I could tell) when Isabelle broke our uncomfortable silence, 'So, explain to me why man has it not in him, in this lifetime, to become what the world needs.'

I thought for a moment, between strokes, finding the words, 'Man's error is in taking his view of the world for all there is; and his view of himself for all he will be. Philosophy, science, psychology, they tell us that this is a farce, and yet the common man clings to this petty and weak illusion fearing the unknown and uncertainty because its beaten into him and he is too weak to stand, too blind to see. What man is not is a fixed or enduring form. We are but always and forever a wonderful transition, a narrow and perilous bridge between nature and the universe, and nothing less. Shrouded in art and religion, shrouded in technology and science, shrouded in good and bad culture and the continuously developing and complicating civilisation is our innermost destiny that drives us beyond what we are, the thing become, and always towards something deeper and more complex, the thing becoming. How man pulled himself up from the Middle Ages and into the brightness of the Enlightenment is nothing short of miraculous, and yet how man has moved from the glorious then to now is surely an embarrassing nightmare. Man is far from a finished creation; rather a challenge to the current spirit, the current vision. That is the truth. A distant possibility but one dreaded as much as desired.'

'Why dreaded or desired?'

'Because between birth and death our life hangs tremulous, irresolute, diluted with false meaning, yearning for a truer calling, a truer time spent experiencing the beauty of nature, of spirit, of life.' I thought about the beast in the dark, the *Treatise*, and how it claimed that there were those, the few, the so-called wolves, who are beyond the security and innocence of the 'civilised' man, whose fate it is to be tortured by the riddle of human destiny. 'There is a way to true being, to the immortals, but too few have it. It starts off an inkling, a doubt, and for a few hesitating steps in his life he will entertain this yearning but will certainly pay for it, either immediately or in the end, with suffering and loneliness. But as for striving with assurance towards the authentic, the genuine, the sincerity of our true being and enduring the journey through the cold wilderness towards immortality, oh, he is deeply afraid of it. Dreaded of it even. Our current culture and measure of things only offers him who tries greater sufferings, greater loneliness, and even though sweet knowledge and eternal truths lie at the journey's end, the desired, he is still not willing to suffer all these sufferings and to die all these deaths. And despite the thousand lives he has up his sleeve, the common man won't dare to risk one of them.'[5]

'And what about you, monsieur? Will you not risk one? Are you not risking one now?' Isabelle smiled softly. 'This is all well and good to describe man from afar, monsieur, but at some point even you must become him and then what will you do with yourself?' She laughed. 'Your thoughts are much too lofty. You have been dreaming this nightmare for too long. Your head swims in the surrealism of your reality and that is both your gift and your curse. You see what others do not see, you feel what others do not feel; this is your perch, your vision of the world, and I'm sure it is as beautiful as it is dizzying, but at some point you must come back down and walk your path, whatever that may be.' She raised her eyebrows knowingly. 'And what good timing; we are here

FOURTEEN
HOMESICKNESS

I STOPPED ROWING and let the paddleboat glide the last few feet, gently coming to rest at the end of a short landing stage of wooden planks. It was low to the water, almost equal height of our paddleboat; I looped the rope attached to the bow around a small timber mooring, stepped onto the jetty and lent a hand to Isabelle.

'What is this place?' I asked now seeing our destination up close; the planked jetty turned to gravel where it met the grassy island, and two paths veered off and away from each other; the left path went towards the house and the other curved right towards the glasshouse. The extravagant home was fashioned out of great slabs of marbled grey slate, lovely dark red brick, and complimented with cream facades; a magnificent green creeper vine covered the entire left side. Although it was indeed a single story house its ceiling sat well over twelve feet high and the roof pitched in several places, the highest of which sat a weathercock. I could see four chimneys (one consumed by the creeper), and guessed it must have had eight or ten rooms. The glasshouse was of equal size though much simpler in design; long and rectangular and pitched in the middle the length of the building.

'I was told,' Isabelle began as we walked along the jetty towards the estate, 'this was the home of a very old woman, a compassionate and kind and worldly woman. Her family owned the adjoining lands, this lake, and this little island, but donated them to the city many years ago. The family home and the glasshouse, however, have always remained private property.'

The air had gotten noticeably colder and the patchwork of heavy grey clouds that had hung stubbornly around the city finally drifted off someplace else, revealing more treasures of the night's sky. Our feet crunched on the gravel pathway and our breath fogged as we walked towards the glasshouse. The path led to the centre of the building where we came upon a large glass and wrought iron gate; it was tall, had twin doors and arced steeply. Iron lettering had been fashioned above the gate; it spelled '*Labyrinthia.*' Isabelle grabbed hold of the iron handles.

'Isn't it locked?' I said.

'Why would it be locked when no one is meant to be here?' She shot me a quick smile and then heaved down on both handles with considerable effort. Iron scraped as Isabelle pulled the large doors open; a whoosh of warm, moist air rushed over us. We stepped inside and Isabelle closed the doors behind us; the fragrance of flowers and soil and wood was overwhelming. The glass ceiling absorbed the moonlight and bathed the interior with a faint white luminescence. I looked around and could see that the glasshouse was tightly filled with an enormous array of flora that appeared to be arranged haphazardly; some plants were potted while others were in long wooden planter boxes, some were on trestle tables with plants stacked on top as well as underneath, and some things had even been planted directly into the soiled ground. It looked almost unkempt and forgotten as some things were overgrown, unpruned, or simply out of place, and yet there was so much organised beauty, so much care, or at least regular watering. It was magnificent and enchanting. I looked at Isabelle, barely containing my wonderment. 'Go,' she said, inviting me to lose myself. I walked around the mazed isles, joyously lost in this secret garden labyrinth, captivated by the assortment and beauty of all this stunning plant life. There were rows of tall white and pink orchids, bushes of puffy orange and red begonias, tables of African violets, a passionflower vine creeping up an iron column and across the glass ceiling, walls of sweet jasmine, wooden barrels full of huge yellow daffodils, clusters of small terracotta pots filled with bright blue hyacinths, stalks of gladiolas in every colour, the roundest dahlias I had ever seen, and across two huge rusted horse carts an entire assortment of fresh herbs (basil, cilantro, watercress, thyme, sage, rosemary, and others too). In the middle of the glasshouse was a large round pond fashioned from wood and iron and dappled with small green water lilies and filled with countless little orange fish; their sudden movement rippling the water and making the moon dance on its surface. I did lose myself, running my fingers through a section of soft ferns, ducking under huge palms, pricking myself on bursting cycads. There were also old and rusted furnishings either placed on purpose or simply forgotten and leaning on something: a marbled sundial, a slatted picnic bench adorned with iron ringlets, wooden wagon wheels with broken spokes.

'*Monsieur*,' Isabelle called from the far end of the glasshouse, 'this way.'

I followed her voice through the garden maze until I came to a small landing that opened up to something breathtaking; a spacious room soaked in moonlight, beautiful red daisy-like flowers clustered in unimaginable number in a low wooden planter bed that ran along all three glass walls, the same ivy creeper that was on the house outside crawled up all four corners and reached out to each other across the glass ceiling, and in the centre of the room sat a huge rectangular daybed, old and carved of thin white wood.

'Isn't it beautiful,' Isabelle said almost in a whisper. She was sitting in the middle of the daybed with her arms folded around her knees, pulling them to her chest. 'Isn't it marvellous?'

I walked around the room running my hand gently through the scarlet flowers; one of the creepers had made its way across the grassy ground and wound its way up the leg of the daybed. Despite the darkness outside I could tell that the view from this room was a stunning vista of the lake and parklands beyond.

'Do you know what they are called, those flowers?' Isabelle said.

They looked like daisies, only their petals were a blood red but the tips a bright yellow. 'No.'

'They are a wildflower known as the *Indian Blanket*. There is a legend about this flower,' she said watching me, 'and the legend tells of an old Indian blanket maker whose extraordinary talent for weaving produced such stunning blankets that members of faraway tribes travelled many miles to trade their pottery, jewellery, and basketry for one of his beautiful blankets. One day, when the blanket maker was getting very old, he realised he had only a short time left to live. He began to weave his own burial blanket, which he intended as a gift to the Great Spirit when they should meet. Determined to make it more beautiful than any he had ever created, he wove into it intricate patterns using his favourite reds, yellows, and browns. When indeed the old blanket maker died, his family wrapped him in this most beautiful blanket. The Great Spirit was so pleased with the exquisite gift but also saddened that his tribe could not also enjoy its beauty, so he decided to share the gift with them. In the spring that followed the old man's death, wildflowers of the design and colours of his last blanket bloomed above his grave and spread across the land forever.'[1]

Isabelle patted the worn, thin white cushion of the daybed, 'Now come, please sit.'

I sat down and found it quite comfortable despite its age. Isabelle closed her eyes and took a few deep, calming breaths; she crossed her legs and folded her hands in her lap. She opened her eyes and laid a gentle smile, 'Now, *monsieur*, it is my turn to speak, and I am going to tell you how it is that I know what troubles you.' Her tone was serious, not solemn but deep and thoughtful, as though she had been collecting her thoughts all night and now was the precise moment to let them out.

'Do you think that you are truly alone? That there is no one at all that understands you? Do I not understand you, now, here, tonight? I only know too well what causes your heart to ache so, your despair, your hopelessness, your fear for not just what the common man does but what he carries on and gives back to this world. Your pain and suffering is beautiful and the time has come to no longer run from it but cherish it. You have felt it too deeply for too long.'

'Why have I?'

'Well, *monsieur*, the person who does not care does not feel pain; you feel pain precisely because you do care, and care so much. And you are right to feel so much pain, right a thousand times over, but still you must perish. You are an artist and a thinker, a man of such splendid depth and awareness for true beauty, already I can see that, always on the path of what is great, sublime, eternal, and never content with what is petty or lacks substance. But, as is often the case for those with a dimension too many, life has awakened in you so much so that you can no longer tolerate the trifling, banal, or mundane, and so stirs your need for greater joys and sweeter fruits well beyond this trivial world of men.[2] But you shall not have them, *monsieur*, not now, not here, not yet.'

'Why?' I said sadly. Now that Isabelle spoke and spoke freely, I found myself hanging on her every word.

'Because you have not yet learnt to breathe and suffocation is a hard death. Most men will not swim before they are able to, and how can they? They are made for land not water! And nor will most men think, for he is made for life, not for thought. And he who thinks too much has sacrificed living for thinking and will one day surely drown.[3] And this is what is happening to you, my sweet *monsieur*, you are drowning. You have gotten so tired and weary of your life, have you not? You have lost your faith in man and his high destiny, become fed up, overtaken by its worthlessness and now find yourself striving for some kind of escape, longing to penetrate to a world beyond this one, to a reality more akin to you and your delicate soul.[4] It is true that that is where you belong, that is your home, and it is that which your heart aches for and why it is you long for death.'

'Is this why you have brought me here? To take me to this other world?'

'No, I have not. Because you know exactly where this other world lies hidden. And in the words of my grandmother, it is the world of your own soul that you seek. Only within yourself exists that other reality for which you long.[5] I can give you nothing that has not already its being within you. So, yes, you must perish, and that time is soon. But just as the flowers bloomed above the old man's grave so you must return, *monsieur*, and give something back to this world for how else do you hope humanity will be enriched if you are not a part of that which comes next, that sweet blossoming, that wave of brilliance? All your pain and suffering will be for nothing.'

Her words pierced and cut to the centre of me; I

felt heavy in my chest, so much so I wanted to cry immediately, but it was almost a giddy feeling, not quite sadness, certainly not (after a moment's thought). Her words so perfect in capturing my wretched predicament but also so sweet, so kind in their knowing, their understanding, their foretelling. Isabelle retrieved a thin silver container from her bag, 'Do you smoke *monsieur?*'

'No.'

'*Bon.*' She opened the little container and inside was three hand-rolled cigarettes; she took one, closed the tin and placed it back in her bag. Isabelle looked at me for a long time, giving me that same searching look she had earlier; her grey-blue eyes striking, her sweet lips just parted. There was that feeling of wonderful strangeness that swirled around us again, an energy that had conspired to bring us together and, well, and here we were, in this most magical of places. Isabelle lit the end of the cigarette, inhaled deeply and closed her eyes in ecstasy. After several seconds she tilted her head back and gently blew a long stream of smoke into the air; it hung above us for a moment like a warm fog and had a peculiar perfume to it, earthly and organic.

'Why is it so hard? Why must we struggle for so long, clamber lonely and lost through our destitution?' I asked.

'Because those who have a dimension too many must venture beyond what the common man knows, out into his own personal wilderness before he can come home. And the glory of his journey is just so because he must do it on his own with no one to guide him. His only guide is his homesickness.'[6]

'But you said that you understood me, that I was not alone.'

Isabelle laughed softly, 'Yes, you are not alone in your pain and suffering, of that the world has plenty of patrons. Too many. But your journey beyond the veil is for you and you only. The treasure you seek can only be savoured by your lips.' Isabelle closed her eyes for a moment before continuing, this time quite solemnly, 'I brought you here to help make your own world visible to you. That is all.'

Isabelle shuffled herself towards me so that our knees were touching. She put her hands gently on the side of my face and held them there studying me. I could smell the laurel and lemon on her wrists, and loose blonde hair gently fell across her moonlit face. I was lost, lost in the stunning surrealism that this night and my life had come to in this very moment, this climax. I thought that nothing more could be asked of fate; that it was now time to take a breath, to breathe one's last and die.[7]

'Not yet, *monsieur*,' Isabelle drew deeply on her cigarette once more, held in its magic, and softly, smoothly, caressingly breathed the smoke over my face in a long steady stream. The warm, grey fog swept over me; it moved like liquid through my body as I inhaled her breath. It filled my mouth, my lungs, my being; I closed my eyes but all the strength had gone out of me to open them again; my head was heavy and I could feel it wanting to sway. My fingertips tingled and my heartbeat slowed to a deep rhythmic throb. Without the energy to speak I slowly laid down on the daybed; it was so soft, so comfortable, I felt like I could sleep for a thousand years.

'Faites des beaux rêves,[8] my sweet monsieur,' I heard Isabelle's voice distantly.

FIFTEEN
ALL THAT I AM

I WOKE WITH A START; that sensation of falling jolting me awake. I sat up, confused, for the moment forgetting where I was, but then the familiar furnishings of my bedroom subsided my disorientated panic. I blinked myself back to a certain reality and checked my watch on the bedside for the time. It was already after midday though I couldn't tell, my shuttered room preserving a fortunate darkness. I slumped back down, headachy, tired, and yet visions of last night's dream flashed in my mind.

Last night's dream... I sat up again and looked over at the empty side of the bed, wondering where she was, or how I even got home. I got up and went into the living room, the drapes were drawn and in the dull grey of my apartment there was no one else but me. I sat down on the sofa and held my head in my hands; the intoxicating journey of last night, of Isabelle Bonnaire, piecing itself together in dreamlike scenes. Places blurred and formed, a boat and a lake, the scent of flowers, phrases echoed in her sweet accent; *I was there*, I realised, it all happened. The art gallery, the train out to the suburbs, the glasshouse... but how could I not remember getting home? It was then I looked up and noticed a little silver container on the kitchen bench; I picked it up and remembered it being Isabelle's. Opening it I found one hand-rolled cigarette and a written note:

To make your own world visible, monsieur, you must step into the cave you fear to enter, a leap you must make for yourself.

Isabelle xox

I thought back on the night and struggled to deny that there was a sense of serendipity that had swirled things into place; my life had unravelled in the last few days and yet I can only submit that I have willed it so for who else decides our destiny but ourselves. Isabelle was right, I had been suffocating, longing for death, for an end to the anguish that was crushing me but this was not an answer, only an ointment.

I knew what needed to be done; I needed to finally let it all go. To find oneself amongst this humdrum and befuddling circus is an almost impossible task. No, a journey beyond where time stops and identity fades, where the mind dissolves and the soul is freed; that is where I must go, alone into that very wilderness of which no one can save me.

I didn't leave my building until it was late in the afternoon; bad weather had plagued most of the day with heavy rain that poured relentlessly beneath dark clouds that hung low and gloomy over the city. Rolls of thunder could be heard somewhere far off. The dirty streets glistened with a wet sheen as the rain fell between buildings; cars splashed through puddles and people with umbrellas darted between street corners. It was too wet to walk to Harvey's so I had to catch the train; the stations were busy with people smelling damp and a little sweaty, eager to escape the deluge.

I reached *Le Gamaar* and noticed the marquee read *Waking Life.* In the foyer some latecomers were quickly helping themselves to the free popcorn and I could see the opening credits rolling on the screen. I went up the stairs to the booth and found Harvey putting the second reel onto the number two projector.

'Hey'.

I sat down in his chair, 'I think I'm going to go away.'

'What do you mean *away*? Where?'

'I'm not sure just yet,' I said thoughtfully.

Harvey shook his head, 'Hang on, I saw you two nights ago, and I know you said you felt like you were on the edge of something, a wilderness, but where'd this come from?'

'Something happened to me last night, Harvey, something... I don't know.'

'What do you mean? What happened?'

I searched for a simple answer, but struggled to find one, 'I don't know how to explain it – just a stunning turn of events, one after the next, and now...'

'And now?'

'Now it's become so clear to me, I can't go on living the way I have; this life I live is not mine; this place, it's not my home. I'm too resentful, too hopeless, and I know that now.'

'And you really think running away from it all is the solution?'

For once I was calm and it was Harvey who couldn't keep himself from being overwrought. 'No, that's just it, Harvey. I'm not running from it, I'm running to it, to the heart of it, to the heart of me. It is just as we discussed two nights ago. Within us and us alone can we hope to find the answers to our owes; the more we look out there for that which we hope to nourish us the more we'll suffer, and the more we let ourselves suffer the more we deny the hollowness that's eating away inside. Its time I finally acknowledged all this discontent and frustration and shiftlessness; and to do that I must embrace it, understand it, love it even! Only then can I come to terms with it, conquer it, and overcome myself. Do you see?'

Harvey's face relaxed, he was realising this wasn't one of my usual idealised rants. 'I get it; to avoid pain and suffering is to fail to recognise that it's a natural part of aiming for and reaching anything worthwhile.'

'Exactly.'

'Mmm.' He still looked uncertain.

'Look, deep down I long for hope and happiness and fulfilment above anything, but I have let adversity and difficulty almost defeat me; I have let the common man and his apathy near drown me. Now I shall use the great pangs of displeasure that have tormented me as the counterpoint of the great feelings of joy I must be able to experience.'

'And that's why you feel the need to go away?'

'Yes. There is nothing for me here, not now, not while I see things the way I do.' I gave a long sigh. 'This is it, this will be my great letting go, and to where and for how long who knows. But that is the leap I'm willing to take, the leap too few make. Our inability to reinvent ourselves is partly what stops us from living wholly fulfilling lives; we're too afraid, too unwillingly.'

Harvey looked at more for a few moments, mulling over what I was saying. 'Well, I can't blame you for wanting to escape this shell of a world. It has a terrible knack for making the few and breaking the many. And to be honest, Will, I can't say this really surprises me either. Probably more just a matter of time.' He managed a wry smile, 'When are you leaving?'

'I'm not sure; tonight, tomorrow, the next day? All I know is the urge to depart has reached its climax. There is nothing else for me to do but go.'

'Well, you'll have to write me a postcard or

something, so I know where you end up.'

I stood up and we hugged our goodbye.

'What about Amy?' Harvey asked.

I thought for a moment, 'Like I said, this is my great letting go. Life goes on and time tells; and our happiness is a measure of how truly we've lived, I suppose. I can't hold back any longer; if there is a deeper purpose somewhere inside me then I'm daring to touch it, whatever the cost.' Harvey nodded his understanding; that was enough, that was our farewell.

Back out on the street twilight was forthcoming but the heavy clouds were grey and moody and made it darker than it should have been. The rain had mostly stopped but everything was still wet and shiny; street lamps flickered on and storeowners shut their shops and turned down their lights. I was suddenly at a loss for how or where I should begin this journey. I fumbled in my pocket and found Isabelle's silver tin; I turned it over in my hand thinking of our night together and the words she imparted. *My only guide is my homesickness.*

I walked through the dark sodden streets and past grey decaying buildings; not so lonely, not so despaired. *All that I am I carry with me*, I thought. A sweet excitement for the unknown settled in my mouth and brought a smile to my face. I had no idea what tomorrow would bring and yet I felt thrilled to be where I was, walking this concrete steppe, not as a starving wolf but as the thing becoming; whatever that was to be.

I boarded the same overland train and headed for not such a forgotten suburb; no honest folk in my cart this time, but a cold draft still. I got off at the end of the line and headed for the same bench with the tree whose branches hung over the wall. I crossed over and entered the park, making my way under the cover of shadows towards the paddleboats whose gentle knocks guided the way. Dipping the oars in that cold, black ink I made my way across the lake heading for the little island with the glasshouse; it wasn't my final destination but it was a start. I tied the paddleboat and followed our footsteps to the glass gates, dare I say with more trepidation than last night despite knowing what was on the inside. I heaved down on the iron handles and felt the warm rush of a place forbidden to those who dared not enter. I walked around the mazed aisles, reacquainting myself with the enchantment of this labyrinth. There was no moon tonight and the glasshouse was dark; I wondered what it would all look like during the day. Eventually, I made my way to that end room on the landing with the daybed and the *Indian blanket* and the creeper vines. I climbed up on the bed and sat with my knees drawn; my mind a torrent of displaced thoughts, an undercurrent of anxiety quietly running beneath it all. This was the fear of the unknown we all have inside us, but it wasn't something that necessarily required you to run from it; just a reminder that you were doing something unexpected, unplanned, and with that goes a certain exhilaration. I pulled the silver tin from my pocket and took out the cigarette; it smelled earthly and organic and it was just me now. I put it shyly to my lips, struck a match and lit the end; it glowed yellow then orange then it was alight and smoking. I took a few short drags; too timid to draw deeply. Then I remembered to let it all go, put the cigarette to my mouth and inhaled long and slow; its noxious, smoky balm filled my lungs and I held it; and the longer I did the more I felt it drift through the walls and enter me; and then I became lightheaded and woozy. It was pleasant though; I felt warm and calm and my eyes watered a little. I lay down on the daybed, relaxed and at ease, staring up at the glass ceiling, beginning to lose myself in a sea of wandering thoughts. I took another long drag, filling myself with its magic; but I don't remember falling asleep.

A thick fog began to fade but my thoughts echoed, bouncing off invisible walls. A bamboo forest surrounded me in all directions; the thick stalks soaring hundreds of feet into the air. The sky was dark and full of stars though the forest seemed bright like daytime. The ground suddenly shuffled beneath me; looking down I saw that I was astride a large beast; it stood strong and powerful but shifted anxiously. It was a huge lion with bright blue fur and a thick green mane, long lashes, dark rubies for eyes, and bright red lips. It had a wooden collar that hung loosely around its neck adorned with little silver bells that tinkled softly, and a lovely red tassel that hung at the bottom. It sidestepped and circled, growling nervously. I made to grab hold of the wooden collar but in my right hand I suddenly gripped a flaming sword that radiated warmth and light. I looked around this strange place and something in the distance amongst the bamboo caught my eye; a small, glowing white beacon of some kind. I leaped down and walked towards the light. There was a large lotus flower floating above the ground, pulsating its white luminescence. I held it in my hand, mesmerised for a few moments, and then ate it. Somewhere, far off, a drum began to beat dimly. The blue lion shifted beside me so I climbed back on, gave it my heels and burst into an instant gallop. We thundered through the bamboo forest like a gusting wind; the lion flying with speed, manoeuvring its way through the forest with deftness and ease. Though, despite our thundering, the forest seemed never-ending as if it were constantly repeating on itself. I asked the lion to leap and within that moment it soared into the air like a bird, sailing above the bamboo tops weightlessly before landing gracefully in a field of tall grass. We waited and the rhythmic drum began to beat faster and louder. The blue lion circled and the earth trembled as though a volcano was erupting. And then it did. Grass and dirt and rock shot into the air as some great demon climbed out from the depths of the earth. It was monstrous in size; it had eleven heads all of different colour (purple, green, yellow, red, etc.) though its main one was black and had the face of a blood thirsty bull with large fangs; it also had eighteen arms and eighteen legs. And in its various hands it held an array of objects: bells, daggers, clubs, spears, a bow with arrows, and so on. It roared and shook and danced with fury, yelling, 'You cannot defeat me!' And so, on a sea of bright green grass under a star-lit sky the battle began. I urged my noble lion to charge, and it did, evading the rain of arrows and spears the demon threw upon us before soaring once again into the air, somehow changing its course in flight and avoiding the monster's arms swinging club and dagger and spear. I slashed and thrust my flaming sword in glowing arcs of fire as the blue lion leaped from limb to limb, never needing to touch the ground. The lion roared and the demon bellowed as we danced our song of death. With each mortal wound the demon took – an arm, a leg, a horn, an eye – little by little it shrank in size. But as it did it became harder to fight. The demon's rage intensified and it moved faster, parrying more and more of my attacks despite missing several arms and legs. We raced through the grass side-by-side, swinging and thrusting, ducking and defending, neither of us able to lay the fatal blow. The blue lion became exhausted and could no longer keep up with the pace of the demon. I jumped off and went at the monster myself. I managed to reduce it down to three heads, three arms, and four legs, but my energy was also ailing. Finally, the demon now the size of a grown man, knocked the flaming sword from my hands and seized me. It gripped its bloody hand tight around my throat and lifted me off the ground, but despite this I smiled warmly at it.

'Why are you not afraid?' It said angrily.

'Because death comes for all who dare to live, but it

is not an ending, merely a changing of worlds,' I said with dream-like clarity.

'So, you admit I have defeated you?'

'No, it is *you* who cannot defeat *me*.'

'But look here, I have caught you!'

'It is not that I am momentarily caught, but that I am utterly free, even in bondage that I cannot be defeated. For I possess something within me, a weapon, beyond this physical world that will destroy you if you eat me. So, go ahead, annihilate us both if you must. But I know there is another world and another life awaiting me. As for you, you are but a wretched demon and will surely perish once and for all.'

The demon laughed with relish, 'I see that you are brave beyond mortal man. Even when faced with death you do not cower.' The monster put me back on the ground, 'A life such as yours demands a path of unlimited possibilities.'

'But don't they all?' I said rubbing my throat.

'No, for our understanding of death emerges solely from the conventions of the world. Only the mind that is able to perceive that death has no intrinsic or concrete existence has transcended it. I submit to you. You have indeed defeated me.'

'Well then, I shall forgive you demon.'

The demon then sat down in the grass and began to meditate. I called the blue lion over, climbed on its back, and once again soared into the night's sky.[1]

SIXTEEN
FOR THAT YOU MUST PERISH

I SLOWLY AWOKE to the faint sounds of water pushing its way out of a metal watering can; the handle squeaking each time it was tilted; its pourer shuffling their feet between drinks. I blinked my eyes open and a blurry, dawn-lit version of the glass-walled room of red flowers and creeper vines came to form. A grey darkness still dimmed the air, the morning for the moment still veiled in an almost foggy hue characteristic of that undisturbed and timeless interval where the day has not yet begun. I sat up on my elbows, the daybed beneath me; I rubbed my eyes and shook off the grogginess of sleep.

'Good morning, young man,' an old, womanly voice called out.

My heart missed a beat; I had heard the sounds of someone but in my sleepiness hadn't fully comprehended it. *Did Isabelle say this place was abandoned or just private property?* I couldn't remember. I looked out into the plant and flower-filled glasshouse, searching for the owner of the voice; I only just caught a glimpse of them moving off and out of sight. I heard the watering can squeak and pour again.

'Don't be afraid,' the old woman said, her voice smiling, 'I don't often get visitors.'

I climbed off the daybed, put on my shoes and with uncertain, hesitant steps walked towards the main glasshouse area. I stood on the step of the landing, peaked in the direction of where the voice came from and there I saw an oldish woman of sturdy stature wearing a worn grey gardening apron overtop a button shirt of dark orange patchwork with the sleeves rolled to her elbows. Her hair was bone white at the root before turning grey then almost black at the ends; although it was cut at her shoulders it was wiry and wildly unkempt. She was giving the puffy orange and red begonias a drink when she gave me a smile, inviting me to go over.

I walked nervously, wringing my hands, not knowing who she was, or if I was going to be in some kind of trouble. I walked down the next aisle so as to stand on the opposite side of the table of begonias. She stopped pouring as I got near and put the watering can down, 'Come, come,' she said smiling, gentleness in her eyes, 'let me see your face.'

'I... I'm sorry for intruding,' I began.

'Oh, fiddlesticks. Don't be sorry. There's no such thing as intruding, or even accidents for that matter. No, there are only the very possibilities we ourselves bring on.' She leaned on the table with both her hands and raised her eyebrows, 'The people we meet, the problems we seek, we call for them because we need their gifts. But you already knew that didn't you? Hee hee!' She raised her eyebrows at me before waving a dismissive gesture. 'Now, let me look at you.' A pair of thin red-rimmed glasses hung around her neck by a fine silver chain; she put them on the end of her nose, raised her eyebrows again and quite overtly looked me over. 'Yes, yes, not a more striking image could there hardly be; a beautiful wolf of the steppes that has lost his way and now strays lonely in the town and life of the herd![1] Hee hee!' She smiled excitedly; it was huge and sincere and beared all her ivory white teeth.

I was too disorientated to hear her properly, too

groggy from sleep, too confused. I looked back towards the room with the *Indian blanket* and the daybed and the creeper vines; I felt disordered and strange, 'Am I dreaming?'

'Well, show me that reality is not a dream. Show me that a dream is not reality. *Heh*, you can't. Anything that your consciousness can touch has the power to transform you; and so everything that your consciousness *does* touch must be real; dream or otherwise. Hee hee. So, you say, 'is this a dream?' and I say, 'does it make a difference?'' She slipped the gardening glove off her right hand, reached across the table and cupped the left side of my face, brushing my cheek with her thumb and looking deep into my eyes. 'Oh my,' her tone suddenly becoming serious, 'such loneliness, such savagery in you too. So restless and homeless, you poor boy. Tsk tsk.' Her voice was melodic but crackly like an old vinyl record. She slipped her gardening glove back on and picked up the watering can, 'Walk with me; I have a bit to do and not a bit of time to do it in.'

'How, how can you see all that?'

'Oh, your tortured soul is made visible in your eyes,' she began quite nonchalantly, studying the various plants and flowers we were passing, 'You see, the great spasms of confusion and despair that torment so many people in this time are in fact the manifestations of some degree of awareness for our situation.'[2]

'What situation?'

'Well, that something of immense proportions is taking place, is always taking place, and fear, anxiety, despair only reveal this repressed awareness.' The light-heartedness and almost airy note of her speech lifted her words despite their weight. I realised this was not new knowledge to her but the expected realities of our circumstances, our actions. She continued with a sigh, 'But sadly, such is the ebb and flow of our human existence as we still make ourselves stumble through so much muck before we find that divine trail for which we have momentarily lost in this time of blindness. And it is during these great periods of recession that human life is reduced to real suffering, to real hell, and it is so because two ages, two understandings, the culture and the civilisation are at last overlapping.'[3] The old woman walked slowly, not for any frailty but for her poise and calmness. 'And it is those people, that generation, whether they realise it or not, that are caught between the *Symplegades*,[4] the clashing rocks of old tradition so deeply ingrained in the minds of the youth that they cannot find their own form or freedom for self-expression. Oh,' she interrupted her stream of speaking putting a hand on my arm, 'I'm not moving too fast for you, am I? I know you've just woken up.'

'No, no,' I said despite the strangeness of it all.

'Good, good. Where was I? Oh, yes, the denial of your opportunity to discover and express yourself! Well, this inevitably leads to the young soul being cast in old moulds; isn't that witty. Their feelings stiffen in old practices, and instead of expanding creatively, they foster hate towards the old way of thinking and the institutions responsible for denying their progress,'[5] she scrunched up her face. 'And *this* is the cause of your torment; you, like many others, are caught between two ages, two modes of life and so have lost the feeling for the beautiful, for the self-evident, for the intrinsic, for being safe and innocent and free to explore. But! *Unlike* many others, you know it's there, you can smell it, taste it, and you're demanding the right to feel it. Hee hee!' She finished her point in palpable excitement and was smiling and squinting with joy.

The old woman stopped to water the gladiolas before continuing in her casual, unflappable tone,

'Naturally, this is not felt equally amongst the population. And that is because justice is not served nor opportunity given nor morality bolstered until those who are unaffected are as outraged as those who are,'[6] the old woman said reminiscently. 'You see, civilisation is the destiny of every culture. The transition from one to the other is not a matter of conscious choice but the eventual and inevitable outgrowing of former beliefs and understandings. And of course this happens at separate times in separate places for separate people. Here, here, look,' the old woman stopped walking and put down the watering can in front of a low table of perhaps twenty or thirty pots of blooming daisies. In her left hand she gently held a stem where at its end a large bud was just getting ready to burst open and let the flower within unfold; and in her right hand she held the stem of a daisy already fully bloomed, and by way of the slightly browning tips of its white petals was perhaps beginning to die. 'You see, cultures are things becoming,' she tugged on the stem with the bud, 'whereas civilisations are the thing become,' now tugging on the daisy flower, 'and so as a culture reaches its peak in art, in intellect, in expression, soon little or nothing new will come from it. It will only expand as a civilisation focused outwardly, expanding yet decaying, and naturally after a time become insincere and artificial, passing on in drab and disconnected forms what was formally beautiful and sublime.'[7] She let go of the stems and raised her eyebrows high.

'Has it always been so?' I asked as we moved on.

'In a way, yes. The growth of humanity is always an ebb and flow; how else does something become old and then something new take its place? The transition takes time because people need to experience it, feel it through and through, before they outgrow it, realise its limitations and eventually improve upon it. What good is the new if you are still enjoying the old? Hee hee.' She raised her eyebrows once again. 'Unfortunately, a big part of life is trial and error, and new doesn't necessarily mean good; and there are still far too many greedy, hateful, and selfish people in this world I'm afraid.'

Finally, the old woman's demeanour flattened a little, 'A man only grows with the greatness of his task, with the demands of his calling. But before he is to succeed he must first have within himself the capacity to grow,' she poked a bony finger in my chest, 'otherwise even the most valuable task or the most worthwhile journey will be of no benefit to him. A man not ready is more likely to be shattered than rewarded.[8] And this is now becoming a grave problem of great peril; man has become so distracted, so entertained, so fixated on the meaningless he has no idea how to discover the meaningful... he has forgotten what it is he came to do, why it is he is living one of his thousand lives.'

'Which is what?'

The old woman stopped suddenly and again grabbed my arm, 'Why did you come here?'

I contemplated my answer, drawing on the past few days, my night with Isabelle and the gravity of her words; then to the *Treatise on the Lost Souls*, and the beast in the dark. I responded meditatively, 'To have my own world made visible to me; to find my home.'

'You mean to finally perish once and for all,' the old woman said without smiling.

'Perish?'

'The ultimate answer that you seek will not be found in intellectual concepts and philosophies, no matter how sophisticated. It cannot be merely told to you. It can only be felt, discovered by a direct and non-conceptual experience of reality,[9] a deeper reality, far beyond what has poorly nourished you so far.'

'*A non-conceptual experience of reality...* H-how?'

The old woman looked at me thoughtfully, 'You see,

you only believe in that which is obviously true, but you do not see that which is obviously possible.'

'Which is what?'

'Oh, well, *anything*. It is merely the logical extension of what you already know to be true. And the possibility of anything lies hidden in the very cave man fears to enter. Hee hee!'

This was all too much, too much to understand, to comprehend, to apply. My head spun and my mouth was dry. I sat down on the edge of the pond to catch my breath; the goldfish scattering. The old woman took pity on me and sat next to me, putting a hand on my knee, 'Don't worry child, we have made life much harder than it was meant to be for ourselves, and for those that are caught between an age, that long to push through rather than submit, the struggle can sadly be too overwhelming, and often is. But! Not so for you, no, your journey is only just beginning. Hee hee.' I watched her stand up and glance around as if looking for something in particular. 'Ah, there it is! Come along, the hour is getting late and it is time I set you on your way.'

As I stood up I realised that the sun still hadn't risen. In fact, the dim greyness of dawn had not broken any more than when I first woke, if anything, it had gotten darker. 'On my way?' I said as I followed her.

'Yes, yes. Come, come,' the old woman said impatiently, imbued with a sudden sense of urgency. We walked our way to the far corner of the glasshouse where we came upon two rows of shrubs three-feet high planted directly into the ground; a narrow, beaten path separated the rows that were about ten-feet long. At the entrance to these shrubs, against the glass panes sat a large wooden workman's bench; it was dark wood, thick, covered in dust and soil, and had a large split that ran halfway through the middle. A creeper vine wound its way up the back leg and across the far corner and a small patch of moss had taken in one of the shallower crevices. On the table were a variety of articles; old rusted gardening tools, stacks of tiny terracotta pots (mostly broken), an assortment of glass jars filled with all types of dried contents: mushrooms, lavender flowers, sticks of rosemary, a jar of red berries, a jar of tangled roots, and others too. Also on the table was a wooden dish with brown and white bird feathers bound together, and sticks of white sage fastened with red twine. The old woman picked up a small handmade wooden bowl and a wooden pestle; she walked over to the shrub, 'Do you know what plant this is?' The shrub had long ovate green leaves and beautiful large, bell-shaped flowers of light purple; it also had little black berries that hung along its stems.[10] The old woman began picking the berries and placing them into the bowl, 'It's the *deadly nightshade*. But such an awful name, tsk tsk.'

'What are you going to do with them?'

'I'm going to make you a tea,' she said, 'a tea so that you may perish, and see.'

'See what?'

She stopped picking berries and turned to me, '*What it is you are looking for*,' she said smiling. 'Anyone who wishes to enter that cave, enter the darkness that lies beyond their consciousness must at first undergo an unravelling, a process of profound shattering transformation, a detaching of their ego, their identity, their everything.'

'And for that I must perish?'

The old woman took a few steps towards me, 'You wish to penetrate that which is beyond you; to plunge into the vast ocean of your unconscious and connect with the inexplicability of its contents is not a task performed lightly, dear child. It is in fact, the forgoing of living. So, yes, for that you must perish.'

And so I watched quietly, and not without

trepidation, the old woman, whoever she was: mystic, seer of souls, shaman, *oko-jumu,* prepare an elixir for my destiny. She moved delicately from shrub to shrub, picking not just the shiny black berries but also one or two of the bell-shaped purple flowers. Then she came to the bench and took ingredients from the jars; a sprinkle of lavender flowers, a pinch of the twisted white roots, one small, shrivelled mushroom, and gently began grinding them all together. The dim grey light that hung in the glasshouse was strange, and dare I say foreboding, for to further encumber this bizarre set of events would be to only point out the obviousness that I myself was finding almost incomprehensible. But no, there was indeed an atmosphere of providence that I was being carried on ever since last night; an air that surrounds those willing to tread a single step outside the mill of common man and lose himself. For who has the will to completely let it all go, to reject everything that they've managed to become or will ever be, and for what? For a glimpse as to why, why any of it. The old woman took an amber bottle from the bench, popped its cork and slowly filled the wooden bowl with a watery-like liquid. She then poured the mixed contents into a little handless wooden cup, put it on the same dish with the brown and white bird feathers and the sticks of sage. The old woman glanced at me sideways, 'Normally, I would ask, 'are you ready?' but you see, they never are, hee hee.'

I smiled, 'How can I be?' Not really asking, but rather readily surrendering.

'Exactly,' the old woman smiled back. 'Come, come, follow me.' She led me back to the room with the *Indian Blanket* and the beautiful daybed and the creeper vine. She placed the dish on the daybed and invited me to sit and make myself comfortable. She drew a box of matches from her apron and lit one of the sage sticks, bathing the leafy end in the yellow flame until the edges caught and it started to smoke. When the sage became aglow she waved it vigorously until the lit ends died down and a steady stream of smoke cascaded its way up into the air, folding itself over and over. The old woman walked slowly around the room, fanning the sage stick and filling the air with an earthly, herbaceous scent coupled with a soft, savoury flavour. I watched her move thoughtfully around the daybed, rhythmically waving the smoking stick of sage, mouthing something inaudible.

As she walked across the glass wall that windowed the lake and struggling light beyond, I once again noticed the diffused amber glow of the as yet still rising sun, 'Why has the sun still not risen?'

The old woman looked at me curiously and then back to the dim, grey horizon, 'Because that, my dear child, is west, not east. It is not morning that breaks but twilight that descends.'

And so it is, the hypnotism of society perverse, the persuasion to fulfil some dreary civic duty or besotted social destiny suffocating, and yet there were times, many of them, that I wished I was under such a spell for this fate of mine is exhausting, and perhaps such a base living is a fruit more sweet than the endless disentangling, searching, and doubting common of my lot (the wolves of the steppes shall we say). But say it is, as this old woman has said, that my lot, at my age, is the very twilight of our great unknown; our fear, our torment, our despair – delirium, confusion, loss, what have you, it all affects us differently – are all the natural anxieties as one stands on that precipice before embarking on a journey none can save us from, our lot, that are beyond the herd, beyond the warm bosom that kept us safe and innocent, beyond the sweet comforts, beyond consciousness and into the void of that unknown of which I have just mentioned. That voyage is saved for us alone, those who are willing to sacrifice so much as we prepare ourselves for that long kiss goodnight and descend into the wilderness of which no one can spare us, of which, only when Helios rouses to break that dark, dreamy slumber for us and summon sweet Dawn and her golden rays, we will be beyond the pain and torment and despair, and bask finally in something warm, not the glory of our fellows, for who, having spent such lonely nights in that forgotten land will need such acclaim, but rather, perhaps a personal glory, a triumph of still not completely understood meaning of his time here, a glorious moment (but which now matters none in the slightest), a conquering of himself and that part that only offers questions without answers, and he will answer questions with more questions and laugh gaily at all he has seen and felt and touched and take comfort in knowing that he does not know, and yet knowing this is far more than most, and that will be his solace, as well as the memory that the darkest place his despair will drag him will still not avail to destroy him but only imbue him with an airy resoluteness of what is beautiful, and of course sublime in this world; the very things we have forsaken, and indeed, perhaps the very things that give rise to the meaning of our lives. This, I now know is what is to come for me, my world about to be made visible to me, my homesickness has brought me here and here I shall dissolve into nothing and yet everything.

The old woman finished fanning the room with the stick of sage and placed it back on the dish. The little glass room was now blanketed in a heavy fog, warm, but also stuffy and rich. The old woman lit a squat tallow candle, giving the room life and light in the now grey gloom of almost night. Our faces glowing and the glass windows melting like watery mirrors; our glimmered reflections captured all around us. She handed me the wooden cup filled with what is to make me perish and prepared herself to say something, clearing her throat and clasping her hands, 'Our consciousness and our reality are not separate, they exist together, as one, in either harmony or disharmony; and we are forever learning how to deal with the graceful fluidity of this relationship within a universal and cosmic context. Within our human journey there is but one lesson that stands above all others; as long as the formlessness and breathtaking freedom of the beyond remain frightening to us, we will continue to dream a reality for ourselves that is comfortably solid, well defined, and predictable.'[11] The old woman closed her eyes and drew a deep breath, her almost youthful ebullience now replaced with a sombre, heavy concern, perhaps a foreshadowing for this voyage I am momentarily to embark on. 'So,' she continued after a few moments, 'as the individual consciousness descends in slumber and rests upon a sea of night and out of which it mysteriously wakes, so too, in the imagery of our dreams does the universe spring into life, enfolding and unfolding effortlessly, only to dissolve once again, timelessly, into the creative energies of the cosmic ocean.'[12]

The old woman's deep, crackly voice gave goose bumps to my arms and filled me with a mystical wonder rarely encountered. I looked down at the little wooden cup and the elixir it contained; it was brown and had bits of root and mushroom floating on its surface. I reflected on her words, and asked, 'The universe is a dream then, and the dream is dreaming itself?'

'Yes, the image is a dream but the *beauty is real.* Can you see the difference?'[13] She finally smiled a half smile. 'Now, please, drink up.'

I held the wooden cup up to my face and my heart began to race; an excitement of nerves reverberated down my body like a rolling wave. My stomach knotted and my throat closed. This is it; this is what I have been longing for, this night, this dream, this moment of madness and clarity. I have been dying a sad and lonely death (a tear rolled), and now here it is, the end, and what lies on the other side I do not know but I do not fear. I held the cup in my nervous and yet excited hands and drank it down in three large gulps. It was horrible tasting; bitter and foul and gritty like dirt. My eyes watered and the acrid, metallic taste made my jaw clench and my teeth shiver in my gums. I felt like retching it back up and had to swallow hard to stop myself from doing so. It was cold and I could feel it move down my chest like a newly formed river carving its way through the banks of my flesh. Once the palpable discomfort was over the old woman smiled warmly, her eyes squinting just; she picked up the dish, took the cup from me and made her way to leave.

'What now?' I asked nervously.

'Relax, and prepare to meet your maker,' she said cryptically.

And with that the old woman turned away and walked out into the now quite shadowy glasshouse. I watched her float into the darkness like a firefly into a cave, the tallow candle's circle of light an ever-receding halo, devoured by the veiling black. I lay back down, put my hands under my head and made myself comfortable.

The unpleasantness brewing in the pit of my stomach slowly subsiding; my breath becoming long and slow and my eyes heavy. The darkness of night now fully descended but with the moon so shallow on the horizon the glasshouse remained almost pitch black. I found myself tracing the outstretched vines of the creeper that were crawling across the glass ceiling; the leaves beginning to tremble as though a breeze was gently blowing through them. The glass panes in the centre that were untouched as yet by the vines began to vibrate from an unknown tremor that seemed to softly shake the glasshouse. Then, right in the centre of the ceiling a single glass pane slowly detached itself from its spot amongst the others, and floated up into the night sky. I rubbed my eyes and beckoned for clarity, but one by one, and one right after the next the square glass panes lifted out of their iron holdings, off and up, as though being gently drawn by some invisible force, and up they went until they were no longer visible. Once the glass ceiling had finished separating piece by piece and then disappearing into the darkness above, the creeper vines seemed to come alive and reach up into the air, swaying softly and glowing a wonderful deep green; a pulsating luminosity produced all by itself. I gaped in awe, my breath caught in astonishment, unable to speak or even produce a sound despite my excitement. I realised then I too felt a weightlessness coming over me, although not a complete disconnection but a slight separating from the dense, physical anchoring of my lethargic, fleshy body to an airy and unbound floating of my conscious awareness. A feeling of such tremendous joy and wonder swept over me; so much so that not just the turmoil of my recent days was all but forgotten, but the turmoil of months and years seemed to recede like a slowly forgetting, foggy dream.

How long it took for the glass ceiling to float away I could not say, but now that it was gone the view to the heavens was open and glorious; the stars became stunningly visible in the dark, moonless night sky, intensifying when I became aware of them. They shined brighter than I had ever seen, and even the soft, clustered sparkle of the Milky Way too slowly made itself visible. When I thought the spectacle could get no more wondrous, little red flowers began to materialise high above me and float down from the sky like tiny, twirling parasols; glowing ruby-red they spiralled softly and silently only a few at a time, but within moments it began to rain these delicate little flowers. They spun and swayed and drifted all around; some landing on the ground, others on the daybed, and some getting caught in the still swaying vines. I was giddy and opened my mouth to laugh but no sound escaped, just a mute expression as I began to lose further touch with my body. The daybed was losing its firmness beneath me too, softening, dissolving, and becoming cloudlike. Then it came, a moment later, the sound of my laughter but only on the inside; young and childlike, innocent and giggly, echoing until it faded. I turned to see where the laughter came from and a saw a young man lying down in the dark surrounded by little red flowers, he was getting further away... I was getting further away. Drifting up and up, into the darkness... I was weightless... boundless... formless

Now I am nimble, now I fly, now I see myself under myself, now a god dances within me.[14]

PART III

SEVENTEEN
FOREST FOR THE TREES

IT WAS THE BEGINNING OF SPRING and the days had begun bathing themselves in that slow warming melt that is so delightful to the skin; though the crisp mornings and cool evenings remain prickly reminders that spring is still the child of winter. Across the still lake beneath the soaring, jagged mountains (whose caps are still covered in snow), a soft mist gathers in ghost-like sheets, sheltering in the shadows of the great rocky curtain that hem this valley in. The clear morning sky, a light blue of almost white presents only a few wisps of clouds; long and thin, dipped in a powdery orange and pink at one end with silvery-white linings at the other. As the sun continues to crest the mountain foreground, it seems to swoll in size like a gooey egg yolk, almost pouring itself over the silhouetted ridge-line before turning from that brooding blood-orange to fiery gold in just a few moments, and so becoming too bright to let you gaze upon its glory. The short, smooth grass that spreads out between my cabin and down to the lake sees the sun's rays earliest and so loses its light frost first. However, the grass that spreads to either side towards the woodland will preserve its deep emerald green and polish of wet dew for another hour or so. Oh, and what woodland! Forests of great cedars interspersed with patches of enormous oaks and maples; their thick dark trunks anchoring to the earth in a tangle of robust, immoveable roots; their bulky bottom branches stretching out ten or fifteen feet in all directions, jutting erratically this way and that way. This dense mix of oak and maple and cedar is most pronounced along the west side of the lake, and provides my cabin grateful refuge from rain and snow alike. The modest timber hut nestled beneath the arms of two tremendous oak branches that arch low over its roof. Further along the southern bank the density of these trees surrender to the towering redwoods that rise hundreds of feet into the sky as though something from the heavens decidedly pulled them up, stretching them like taffy. Their reddish-brown trunks rising above the tops of the dark green foliage of the cedars for about two miles. It must be said, this is nothing as comparable to what lays across the shore on the opposite side of the lake; from my cabin in the west all around to the north grows such a wonderful assortment of conifers: Douglas-firs and white firs, bushy cypresses, short stubby junipers with gnarled and twisted trunks, tall pines and thick hemlocks, luscious spruces and yews. A most lovely array of all the shades of green imaginable, but there, right in the middle of that forest, as though one were looking upon an exquisite landscape oil-painting of greens and browns someone has taken a razor to the work, scratching a section of the woods away leaving only the stark white canvas beneath... Well, here, for reasons only nature can attest, stands the finest grove of the whitest birch trees one ever did see. Their slender, pale trunks, barely dappled, stand fine and erect; the canopy they produce, which begins no lower than ten feet from the ground, radiates the most spectacular lime green of such luminescence one would not be mistaken to thinking that it was somehow artificially lit. But needless to say it is not; this beacon of jade on pallid, ivory stilts is merely the magic one finds with astonishing regularity out here, in nature, that place unspoiled by man, where, right next to you, chickadees, wagtails, and pipits frolic in the drying grass, foraging for insects stirred by the morning sun; or the red-headed woodpecker, from deep inside the cedar forest, calling out *tchur-tchu, tchur-tchur* and drumming his beak, claiming his spring territory... and then a moment later, from further within the woods, another *tchur-tchur* followed by a softer drumming; his rival beating a reply. But something catches your eye and makes you start; three, four, no, five beautiful black and brown butterflies float past your head haphazardly, as though dangling from a string, their flight path curious and carefree. Then, calling across the lake from that grove of stunning white birch I just mentioned come the extravagant singsongs from a family of larks that have nested there; their melody is high-pitched, lisping and tinkling, finishing in a warbling, ascending trill. Their song chimes out across the lake, each note dancing on the light spring air. A chorus of male blackbirds nearby sing their rejoinder in varied and melodious fluted warbles. A series of plonks and splashes momentarily disrupts the early morning symphony as a raft of wood ducks hit the water across the lake; there they will spend their day paddling about the thickets of reeds that grow densely beneath the sagging willows that hang lugubriously at the waters' edge.

I could not tell you how long I have been here; perhaps too long and yet, oddly, not long enough. Everything here feels so familiar, though I cannot recall when I arrived. There is no one else here but the trees and the lake and the birds and the trout. Days pass and I feel no longing, no sadness, no despair – all that a distant memory; I feel only an undisturbed potential. Though something has developed, a little itch, a gnawing that there is something I am meant to do, a place or a person I am to see. But until this apparition of thought takes on form I spend my days in peaceful contemplation; walking through the forest, absorbing its timelessness, awed by a patch of stretching moss or captivated by the patterned intricacy of a fallen pinecone.

I rarely ventured far during the cold heart of winter; instead remaining in the sanctuary of my cabin, warmed by the open fire, sheltered from the howling winds, but accompanied by the Russians and their obsession with the fatalistic preclusive nature of our lives: *Brothers K, Fathers, Souls, The Steppe,* and the best of them all, *Sketches.*[1] The short days and long nights made bearable by such high art, such poetry of life and times and landscapes; romantic in their nihilism, bleak in their hope, and yet flawless in their visions of that which is undeniably, passionately human. And to them do I owe a debt that can never be repaid. But it wasn't until the seasons changed that my mood followed, and so too the activity.

This spring air has a sweet freshness to it, filling me with a vigour long forgotten. I walk for miles through the forest under the dappled, translucent canopy; watching, reading, dozing. It's a strange thought that what strikes one most deeply in solitude is not separation or loneliness, but in fact, quite the opposite: such deep connection. And a connection to nature no less, that origin of origins, forged eons ago in stunning simplicity which without, these reflective thoughts or feelings of wholeness would not exist. Fascinated as much by the experience as the thought that as I walk through the forest of giant redwoods or the grove of ivory and lime birch that I am no longer the same person who emerges from it; that the presence, the smell, the vision, the *relationship* between myself and forest is forever. That the moon and the stars and each and every dawn or twilight, each note the lark sings or the clean swoop and charming hop of a wagtail, all conspire in their moments to share themselves with me, and that my profound appreciation is what compels the beauty to be resonant. That I will go on existing in one of a thousand different ways and yet each of those possibilities will carry with it the deeply felt bedazzlement and supreme magnificence of the universe as it swirls and flashes, bursts and creates itself in ways that are beyond my comprehension, but not and never beyond my intense gratitude.

Enough daydreaming; I returned to my morning chore. *Crackkk!* The split wood toppled gently. I placed another small log on its end, stepped back and swung. *Crackkk!* I repeated this routine now with mechanical exactness; the muscles of my arms, shoulders and back had grown to the task, flaring with the familiarity of the movement. *Crackkk!* I stopped a moment to catch my breath and watched a soft, warm breeze sing its way through the forest and ripple across the lake; the water shimmering as the sun, now fiery gold, casts silvery reflections across the iridescent cobalt and turquoise water. The trees, the trout, the birds, the bugs; everything was awake and bursting with a new day's joy. I looked down at the handle that was stained with sweat and blood, though my hands no longer bled; it was indeed a wonderful task and I chuckled gaily to myself at the thought of it.

I heard a voice, a whisper through the trees, 'Show me your face...' it seemed to say. I looked around but there was no one; nor had there been anyone on the other occasions. The hairs on my neck stood up and that gentle gnawing in my stomach returned. Wiping the sweat from my brow I decided I had enough wood for the week and left the axe embedded in the stump... and left the whisper hanging on the breeze.

It was becoming another fine day; the sun slowly making its way across a cloudless blue sky, serenading this retreated corner of wilderness in a silently warming song. I carried the logs inside, the wooden floor creaking as I stacked the pieces beside the fireplace. Streaks of sunlight shone between the gaps of timber and open windows, catching spectres of dust dancing in the morning light. The cabin was modest in size but was more than adequate; there were no private rooms, just an open square plan where one part of the dwelling overlapped with the next. Nothing was new; it was all creased or cracked, split or sagging, and yet sturdy and comfortable all the same. In front of the fireplace sat a large, irregular piece of driftwood that acted as a coffee table, and placed around it was a black leather sofa with wooden trim and two matching armchairs. The bedroom area stood off to the left where a timber frame (the type constructed for a wall in a home) offered a kind of see-through separation; the framework doubled as shelving and held an assortment of things: stacks of books, trinkets from the forest (a pinecone, some feathers, a small dried bouquet of sunflowers), some interesting rocks and crystals, a couple of candles, and so on. The bed, positioned against the back wall, was large, old and surprisingly comfortable. Opposite the bed on the front wall and somewhat next to the front door sat a sizeable wooden desk with a *Hermes Baby* typewriter, a small potted maiden hair fern, and a few more candles and books (the Americans: *Hem, Faulk, Fitz, Beck*, and a few others[2]). On the other side of the fireplace was a rather basic kitchen; a long, wooden bench top, some cupboards, an oven and stove worked by wood or coal, and an old white, porcelain trough for a sink that sat beneath one of the windows (there was a small water-tank behind the cabin that offered brief bursts of running water). A large, wooden dining table with mismatched wooden chairs finished the kitchen.

I stood in the silhouetted doorway and took in the

view; the brightening grass, the thinning trees between my doorstep and the water's edge, the silvery-blue lake beseeched by a luscious forest all around, the birch, the willows, the crowning mountains... and that gentle gnawing.

Since I came here in late autumn (I remember the oak and maple trees bare and ghostly without their foliage, the great rushes of brown leaves that blanketed the forest floor, scuttering loudly when the winds gusted, and then the light snows that followed), I hadn't yet swum in the lake but dreamt of warmer days when I could. Well, here they were. I walked down to the water and out onto the short, rickety jetty. I shielded the glare from my eyes and watched trout leisurely swim by in the sandy shallows. I undressed, and felt the warmth of the wooden planks under my bare feet. There was a square, timber pontoon that floated in the lake about a hundred-feet out; it must have been anchored for there was nothing tying it to shore. The water looked cold. I dived in and swam out below the surface and came up with a gasp and blew the water from my face. The chill went straight through me but treading water seemed to make it better. I paddled loudly over to the pontoon, fighting the cold, and pulled myself up. I rolled over onto my back, breathless, smiling like a child; I could feel the sun already thawing my cold skin. Laying there, staring up at an endless blue sky, water dripping off the edges of my body, feeling the gentle drop and lift of the swell, I burst into a sudden fit of laughter. It felt good to laugh; to laugh at everything and nothing at the same time, as though none of it really mattered in the end. I sat up, the sun warm on my back, and looked around the valley; never had I seen it from such a spot. The trees all looked a little different, the cabin much smaller, the world was out there – before me, around me. I felt like I was in the centre of it all. I laughed again.

After a while I stood up, gripped my toes on the edge of the pontoon – tipping it with my weight – and dove. I swam down with my eyes open as deep as I could go; the water looked dark and green from below, but the sun penetrated the surface in long shards of shifting white light. The pontoon made a dark shadow and I could see a chain fastened beneath it descending into darkness. The rush for oxygen came but I waited a few more moments, savouring the silent stillness of this murky underworld. I came up through the lightening water and broke the surface with a loud, involuntary sigh. I floated on my back for a minute or so, the sun warming my face, and feeling inexplicably alive. Finally, I turned over and quietly swam breaststroke in. I climbed back onto the timber jetty and lay there until the noon sun dried me.

I spent the afternoon in a pleasant daydream; a faint breeze disturbed the mild spring air, the woods alive with chirps and tweets, and the blue sky slowly filling with piles of fluffy, white cumulus clouds. Evening arrived before long and the cicadas started their noble call, singing their twilight song; their mantra peaking in unison before trailing off in a decrescendo only to surge again like the constant rolling of the ocean's waves. Then it was the fireflies turn, appearing out of nowhere like little flames floating in the breeze. One by one they ignited, as though telling each other it was time to dance. I gazed at them through the window from my desk, drifting like tiny pixies through the trees and across the lake, performing their nightly bedazzlement. I watched a wandering firefly drift through the open door, guiding my guest in; he had a familiar face.

EIGHTEEN
SNOW FALLING ON THE WINDOWSILL

'Hello,' he said, nodding politely, 'I hope I am not intruding?'

I stared a moment before my voice came, 'No, of course not.' At last that gnawing had become something, and here it was. 'I... I've been expecting you, I suppose.' I said somewhat hypnotically.

'Oh! And how did you come to expect such a thing?' He asked smiling.

'I'm not sure; just a feeling I guess.' That's what it was. 'That there was a point to coming here.'

'Coming here and staying so long?'

'Why – how long have I been here?'

'Oh that doesn't really matter. What does matter is

you stay until you understand why it is you came.'

It was suddenly clear, 'And that's why you're here...?'

'That's right,' he said, 'you've been waiting to be told what you've known all along.'

'Which is what?'

'That you cannot know what you don't already have the capacity inside you to know.' He took a step forward and spoke very deliberately, 'I am here to remind you that what you are basically, deep, deep down, far, far in, is simply the fabric and structure of existence itself.'[1] He spoke with a calm reassurance; equanimity that only comes with the reflected clarity of bringing the kaleidoscope of countless lives he had endured into focus and understanding.

He smiled warmly, 'May I suggest we have a drink to loosen ourselves up?' He said waving a tall, unlabelled bottle, 'I have a feeling it's going to be a long night.'

He moved about the cabin with a strange familiarity and comfort; his face casting reminiscent glances. Eventually he made his way to the kitchen and took two mismatched jars from the shelf and poured a third of a glass in each. I lit some kindling in the fireplace and stacked a couple of logs before joining him. We each pulled a chair and sat across from each other at the kitchen table. He stared fondly at his drink; I stared intriguingly at him.

Night had arrived and darkness gently laid itself over the wilderness outside, though the little cabin glowed from within. The flames danced around the room; in our eyes, in our drinks, all the while crackling with mirth. Eyes closed he took a long, slow swig and gave a pleasurable sigh when he was done. The fine liquid had the appearance of diluted honey, and had a sweet, fresh odour to it. I took a sip and found it to be perfectly flavoured with a delightful tartness; it tasted like plums.

'So,' he began, 'show me your face.'

That question; that question I've heard time and again. 'What face? Why do I keep being asked that question?'

He looked into me, or through me; I couldn't tell. But he gave no answer. 'Tell me, why are you here? Can you remember?'

It took a few searching moments to recall, to redraw upon those long forgotten feelings that have brought you somewhere so far from where you started, so far along that path to perdition that we all march to, until that is, he opens his eyes, rings the bell and jumps off, and finds himself somewhere new and undiscovered. That is why I am here; this place was an escape from that, a sanctuary from the world that has greatly misunderstood itself; a reality away from reality.

'I realised,' I began slowly, 'that until man loses himself, he never really begins to be alive. Possessions, property, his reputation, his position – all these things he grasps onto anxiously in a vain attempt to build some arbitrary, culturally acceptable image of himself. But he forgets that without introspection, without self-exploration, without real abandonment it is impossible for him to become fully whole until he has first come to terms with whom his true self is and what it wants.' I cleared my throat, thinking for the words. 'As a result the common man only achieves a poor imitation of the wise man's behaviour because he has not gone through the necessary stages. And as rational or well-lived he may think he is, his mind is still a veneer above a muckheap, that hollow attempt to mimic self-awareness by wearing its clothes.'[2]

The fire crackled quietly and my guest nodded agreeably.

'But the fact is,' I went on, 'most of us will not, and probably cannot reject the cultural norms and value systems we depend on despite how limiting, suppressive or hopeless they may be. And yet by some process of 'going through the mill,' of enduring great periods of difficulties, we ironically wear them as proud badges of adulthood, of graduating through maturity, pretending to ourselves that constant self-frustrations throughout life were in fact important developments of personal growth. Just like the Church and its priests who pander to peoples' hard roads; their sermons have such bleak and depressing undertones, and seem to motivate action only through shame or guilt or fear. If good will and good nature are driven by such measures – that doesn't make one morally upstanding, it just makes one shallow and self-serving. All that is really being offered is an ointment for the ego's hurt pride – an ointment upon which our egocentricity thrives with great vigour.[3] The little and not surprising optimism that it does provide is to accept any ill-fate as though it has some hidden purpose in order to make your situation more tolerable, or to be regularly reminded of your pain and suffering as though that will somehow make you stronger, when in truth, continuing to drudge up the past only succeeds in keeping you there.'

I was surprised at how these notions came flooding

back to me; and yet they came with a calm clarity and simple matter-of-factness. I realised these social issues no longer aroused that simmering spite they once did despite nothing really changing, nothing except the way I perceived it all. All my frustrations, all my anger, all that dissatisfaction, they weren't solving anything; they just created a scaffolding to look at things from a counterpoint. A different perspective, despite how undesirable, that saw through the guises of an artificial world and the skewed narratives it tells people to think, feel, and believe.

'Yes, well,' my guest spoke up after a moment, 'it is sticky subject religion, isn't it? Since the beginning of mankind we have sought for some sort of divine or cosmic answer to our peculiar place in this stupendously inexplicable scheme of things. A fascination that has resolved itself to endure ancient civilisations, take on a multitude of forms, and replace itself over and again, and yet, after all this time, after all its adjustments and improvements, it still somehow falls short on delivering what it promises. And yet the curiosity still remains.' He raised his eyebrows. 'So, as sticky as the subject is it is perhaps the best place to start because unless we work out what should come *after* religion, mankind will continue to conjure up some magical reason for it all, write it down and then shed blood over the grammar.

'You see,' he went on, 'religion is not the same as belief; religion is doctrine, it is dogma, it is language and it is symbols, but all of these things are only vehicles of communication and it is a mistake to take them as the final term or absolute meaning of their reference. They are only convenient means to accommodate a general understanding irrespective how glorious or impressive the preaching. The failure of the follower is to attempt to read or interpret what is being said as the final thing forgetting that this 'final thing' is merely the interpretation of someone else interpreting someone else, and so on, and so on.[4] And yet, if we are indeed all God's children then He should speak to us all equally; the pastor of a local church group should hold no less reverence than the Pope of Rome for there is nothing in their holiness that separates them. And yet there is, but not because of any divine intervention but because of what people collectively make these people to be.

'So, what am I saying? Be wary of he who says he understands God and that you should be doing such and such with your life because he is filling his cup from the same fountain as everyone else, and while everyone else is drinking water he will claim he is drinking wine. And why does he claim he is drinking wine? Well, because he knows the scripture through and through and it has enamoured him with all that it says; his worldview is seen through, and limited by, the yellowed pages of book written centuries ago. But what he has forgotten is that what he has read was foremost a doctrine, a set of guidelines, and – because he still lives in a state of worship in need of forgiveness – he has clearly failed to become the virtuous, godly man it suggests we can be. If he did, well then he would put this instruction manual down having no longer any need of it for he has become the thing beyond his sinful, imperfect self. But he hasn't, nor has anyone else who feels compelled to live their life in constant worship and fear of a vengeful God.

'And herein lays the trap in being fixated on the doctrine, and any doctrine for that matter, as opposed to being enlightened by its messages. This is why one can suggest that the doctrine is like a finger pointing at the moon, and one must take care not to mistake the finger for the moon. And when you look around and see that there are a tremendous number of so called religious people but who lack even the most fundamental of moral virtues, well then, it is quite obvious that too many people suck the pointing finger of religion for comfort and forgiveness instead of looking where it's pointing. Religion, with all its configuration of ideas and rules and practices, is clearly altogether a pointing, and it certainly does not point at itself for the ultimate answers – especially when everything seems to be a parable or a metaphor or a figure of speech intended to elude to some deeper meaning. And nor does it even point at God! For the notion of a God goes hand in hand with the tenets that proclaim it as its figurehead. So, one could say that what religion in fact points to is simply reality, or that it points at one's true self, or the eternal now, at the nonverbal world, at the infinite and ineffable; any or all of these things.'[5]

He took a sip of his drink. 'It's quite comical isn't it? So long, then, as we think about God, talk about God, seek God, there is no God to be found. And why do we look so hard? Because Western culture is so hooked on the idea that there is a formula for success, or a formula for happiness, and for the pious a formula for salvation – conveniently jotted out in that dusty old instruction manual – that will necessarily save them from all sorts of misery in life damnation thereafter. And unfortunately, all political propaganda, certainly all advertising, and sadly most of what we call education is based upon this 'there is a way' method, and that the stricter you follow it the more guaranteed the result.[6] Well, if it was that easy then the world would be full of happy, successful, virtuous people but that is hardly the way things are. And the more competitive things get, the more complicated we become, and the more we continue to rely on out-dated value systems, well, the harder it becomes to pull ourselves out of this mess we're sinking in.

'I know I'm harping on about all this religion mumbo-jumbo but it's important to understand how we've misconstrued it so badly if we are going to put another vision in its place.' He refilled our glasses, planning his next words. 'Have you heard the expression 'the watched pot never boils' or 'tomorrow never comes?''

'Yes, I think so.'

'Well, this is the trouble with the stubbornly religious; they spend so much time and energy looking, waiting, hoping for God that they fail to see the activity. What is the activity? The rivers flow, the flowers bloom, the snow falling on the windowsill. The obvious question is: is this the activity of God? Perhaps. But if anyone watches it in order to see God he will surely be disappointed. And this is why even the *idea* of God is also just a finger pointing to the way of reality, but little do people realise that the whole thing collapses when you try and join God and reality together, to identify one with the other, to find the former in the latter; they are trying to join together two things that were never in need of being joined.[7] Hence, the decaying of religious thought and practice in the more enlightened parts of the world; the gradual realisation that religion is a confusing, bumpy, and rather problematic way of achieving spiritual happiness only goes to show that we've mistaken the ox for the cow, the finger for the moon, religion for reality.

'But because we've had this over-arching Christian sense of reality throughout modern history, this great external as well as internal battle of good overcoming evil, it remains with us in various forms so strongly despite the flourishing post-Christian intellectual climate of today that we struggle to accept any alternate view of reality as more than an inspiring hallucination.[8] Both political and cultural coercion as well as our induced fear of the unknown prevents us from letting go of our omnipotent father figure despite how cruel and immoral the notion of him we know to be.'

'So, what you're saying is we need to look *beyond*

religion, even God, and discover the reality that lies there? Something like this would be the replacing vision, man's place in a greater universal context?'

'Yes, exactly! But not somewhere out there, my dear boy, but right here. And it's always been here, right under our noses, right *inside* of us. The nitrogen in your DNA, the calcium in your teeth, the iron in your blood, heck, the carbon in *apple pies* – these elements were forged in the interiors of collapsing stars billions of years ago.[9] This we know. These building blocks are out there, in space, in other planets, in other stars, *as well as* right here on and in everything we see, touch, smell, and feel on Earth. We are made of starstuff, my dear boy. And in that sense, is the universe not permeating within us? Are we not the universe personified and self-reflecting? Awed by the stupendous magnificence of its symphony of sounds and colours, its depth and scale of inventiveness? Through self-reflexion, not just of ourselves but more importantly of the rich world around us, we allow the universe to feel and know itself. It is made aware of itself through *our* awareness;[10] this point has been reached so that the inexplicable beauty of nature is finally aware of how glorious it is.' He leaned forward across the table, 'You and every other human being are the contents of those collapsed stars brought into a form of being, billions of years in the making, which enables life to reflect on life. Is that not that amazing?'

He could see me brain ticking over, fighting to keep up with these grand concepts. 'So, then, what is the meaning? What is the point of the universe knowing itself?'

'Oh, that will come but don't think about it just yet or you will stumble on how practical theses notions are or aren't. For what is the value of the universe? What is the practical application of a million galaxies? You could hardly say there is one except perhaps simply to enjoy the view![11] No. Just know this; *we are* the universe looking at itself from billions of points of view, points that come and go so the vision is forever new. What we see as death, empty space, or nothingness is only the trough between the crests of this endlessly waving ocean;[12] a universe alive and bursting in unfathomable creativity.'

He inhaled deeply and looked into his drink before finishing it. 'Let's take this outside, shall we,' he said grabbing the bottle.

It was dark and the air was fresh and cool and smelt rich with earthly tones; the cabin aglow with golden light behind us. We walked down to the short, timber jetty and sat with our feet hanging off the edge. We filled our jars with the plum wine and sat in silence for a long while. The cloudless night gave way to a speckled starlit sky; the crested moon reflecting brightly in the still lake. An occasional splash drew my eyes from the heavens quickly to where a trout gulped at the surface, leaving behind a series of perfect ripples. And then, as if serenading us, a lone nightingale began to sing the most delicate song of such sweet whistles that neither my guest nor I dared to speak. But eventually he did.

'You see, life and reality are not things you can have for yourself unless you accord them to all others.[13] They do not belong exclusively or physically to particular persons like kings or queens or empires, and for that reason nor do they belong to particular sets of beliefs or religions. Look up there, the moon doesn't belong to the night sky, or the stars to the infinite black space around them; remove one or the other and the reality disappears. They depend wholly on one another.

'And the same applies for us. You see, separateness is an illusion for everything in some way or another belongs to everything else. Every this goes with every that. Without others there is no self, and without somewhere else there is no here, so that – in this sense – self *is* other and here *is* there. When one comes to this realisation, when you place yourself not at the centre of all that matters but simply as a drop in the ocean, a delicate, contributing part of it, that moment is at once exhilarating as well as a little disconcerting. There is the sensation that it is happening all on its own, that you have lost your grip on what you had always taken for reality, that you are no longer doing it yourself and you wonder, distantly, if you will lose it. And that is because there is a certain passivity to the sensation, as if you were a leaf blown along by the wind until you realise that you are both the leaf and the wind.[14] Experience and experiencer become one experiencing, known and knower one knowing. Each organism experiences this from a different standpoint and in a different way, for each organism is the universe experiencing itself in endless variety.'[15]

I realised this is how he had to explain it all; deliberately, clearly and without pause. Everything made a certain sense that would only become clouded if he tried to elaborate on it any more than he did; for there is a certain clarity preserved when something is expressed as simply as it should; and finally understood as it is or not at all.

'Are you still with me?' He smiled before taking a sip of his drink.

'Yes, I think so.'

'Then let me tell you a story about a Buddhist monk who lived long ago: one day he decided that he knew not the true nature of reality – the physical world around him – and so of course could not appreciate its true beauty. And so he went into the woods set to meditate until he saw the world as it is rather than how he happened to see it. Before he retreated into his cave he took one last look around, and what did he see? He saw mountains as mountains, rivers as rivers, and trees as trees, but sadly didn't feel the slightest wonderment. So, into the cave he went to meditate. Some time passed and a stunning thought occurred to him and so he stepped out of the cave to have a look around. And to his surprise he no longer saw mountains as mountains, rivers as rivers, and trees as trees. He saw nothing; just a wash of shapes and colours. 'Aha,' he thought, 'now I am getting somewhere.' Realising that sometimes to know is actually not to know, and not to know is actually to know, he went back into the cave to meditate further. After some more time passed and when he became thoroughly enlightened he stepped outside. It just so happened that it was dawn and the sun was rising above the tree tops and the monk fell to his knees with tears of joy streaming down his face for he finally saw once again the mountains as mountains, the rivers as rivers, and the trees as trees.[16]

'You see, before we can truly appreciate the magnificence around us in all its glory, in all its beautifully changing individuality, we must first realise its unreality, its formlessness to which *we* give it form. That is to say, when things are considered by themselves, as these isolated, permanent or self-sufficient entities, ourselves included, they become meaningless and dead. Everything exists because of everything else, and it does so in such ineffable dependence and harmony that we are often blind to it.'[17]

'And so one might say that what this monk came to realise is that when a certain enlightenment or appreciation or understanding is reached by the consciousness, one *feels* the force of the universe at work in everything he sees or thinks or feels. And this irrevocable realisation gives a powerful and liberating impulse to his spirit. He has let himself go, like the leaf in the wind, and freed himself by becoming both the formed and the formless, by ultimately freeing himself from himself, which is the only thing that ever bound anyone.

'So, what does this mean for you, my dear boy? The fact is that because no one thing or feature of this universe is separable from the whole, the only real you, or self, is the whole.[18] And for many, the inconceivable truth is that the whole thing is one single, formless, inseparable, cosmically connected entity.'

'The fabric and structure of existence itself...' I said reflecting. His words drove especially deep as we sat beneath the twinkling of a million stars, the shifting silhouetted tops of the distant trees, the moon passing by so slowly... it was all conspiring; it was seeing itself, I realised.

'That's right. What's more is that we cannot ask if the part is creating the whole, or the whole is creating the part because the part *is* the whole. And this is the entire point, whether we call the living universe a 'collective consciousness,' or 'God,' or simply 'the consciousness of all things,' it doesn't change the situation.[19] The cosmos may as well be an everlasting dream of such stupendous beauty and ineffable creativity that true reality simply cannot be reduced to any definitive terms or knowable means; it can only be experienced, felt, cherished.'

He looked at me smiling, 'A lot to take in, I know. But all things you were ready for otherwise you would never have come here.'

'And how's that?'

'You came here to become more aware, of the here and now, the magic that surrounds you, by feeling it, being sensitive to it! Remember, for some great idea, experience or image to take hold of you from the outside and become truly resonant, you must first understand that it is only able to do so because something inside of you responds to it and goes out to meet it. What appears to come to us from the outside can only become visible to us and made our own if we are capable of an inner understanding,[20] an appreciation that recognises not just the beauty of whatever it is but its inseparability with everything else, its reason for happening. That is when we are able to appreciate the cosmic significance of the mountain being the mountain.'

'Or the snow falling on the window sill?'

'Exactly, my dear boy. Only by removing our anxious grip that fastens our egocentricity to our self-centred worldviews and establishing ourselves within the greater unfolding universal whole can we begin to discover the meaning and significance of ordinary things.'[21]

'If, then, there is this basic unity between self and other, individual and universe, how have our minds become so narrow that we don't know it?'

'Quite simply really; in part it's the reality that we've discovered so far; it should be no surprise that our belief systems are direct reflections of how much we know about the world around us. What's unfortunate is that as a society we are gathering scientific knowledge much faster than we are gathering the wisdom to go with it.[22] And secondly, our current understanding of reality is also one that many people want to continue to see and hold onto; it's simple and makes sense to them, and for a lot of people it provides good enough reasons, despite how flawed, for the way life is and how they should accord themselves. And in this sense it offers a perspective that is predictable and safe, that is able to be separated into not just good and bad but separated into physical parts.'

'Fragmented.'

'Yes! And not realising that it is this very hallucination and propensity to fragment that prevents us from experiencing the full intensity of the universe and our consciousness.[23] The mind constructs a concrete reality for us out of the raw material of the universe; but the raw material is fundamentally energy... it can be almost *anything*. There is a sublime world out there of such surreal and breathtaking beauty that we deny ourselves the vision of because we are too afraid to see it.

'What is the universe but an endless ocean of lapping energy of which we are every bit a part of. We are not objects; we have no solidity. We are perceivers, an awareness, orientated by a consciousness that is fundamentally boundless – as boundless as a wave in the ocean. Our perception of objects and solidity is merely a convenient means to navigate ourselves. Suns and planets, oceans and whales, butterflies and summer breezes are just some of the creative life forms of the universe, and it is the presence of our consciousness that gives the appearance of matter, space, time, and of course our brains to perceive it all through. But we are failing to realise that this too is a concept, a description as a way of seeing things that we have taken to be absolute, and in doing so have entrapped the totality of ourselves in a vicious cycle from which we rarely emerge in our lifetime.[24]

'For man to be able to live he must either be blind to the infinite, or have such an explanation of the meaning of life as will connect the finite with the infinite.'[25] He picked up the bottle and gave it a shake, '*Huh*, all finished,' he said not disappointedly. 'Perhaps a good thing too, dawn is approaching and I dare say you've had enough medicine for one night.'

We both chuckled and stood up stiffly. There were still stars in the sky but the moon had gone over the edge long ago and beyond the mountains a dark blue began to emanate faintly. We walked back to the cabin; it smelt musky from the burnt wood and red embers amongst white ash clung to a fading warmth.

'What now?' I asked exhausted and yet still eager for more.

He laughed, 'Now it's time to sleep, my dear boy. In a few hours it will be a new day and with it a new set of questions.' He lay down on the sofa and made himself comfortable. 'Don't worry, I'll still be here when you wake up. You and I are not quite finished.'

NINETEEN
NOBILITY IS LIKE HEAVEN

THE DISTANT SOUND OF CHOPPING WOOD woke me. I opened my eyes to the mid-morning sun beaming in through the open windows, filling the wooden cabin in shades of light and dark browns. I sat on the edge of the bed still waking up; the soft thud of the axe starting up again.

I went outside, marching across the warm grass, 'What is your name?' I asked when I reached him.

He was breathing hard and sweat dripped into his eyebrows. 'My, my, I forgot how good it feels to do this,' he said ignoring my question.

He had cut enough wood to last the summer. 'What is your name?' I asked again but he looked at me as though he didn't know the answer to my question.

'Well,' he said finally, 'does it really matter?'

I didn't answer him.

He leaned on the axe like a walking stick, 'My name is whatever you want it to be.' He flashed a smile but I paid nothing in return and he realised. 'My name is the universe. My name is nothing. My name is your name.' He raised his eyebrows, 'See, it doesn't really make a difference.'

Something in me surrendered. I couldn't tell you why but for some reason that answer seemed enough; more than enough. Like most of what he had said the night before, there was so much in it, so much explanation and answers and yet, his simple words seemed not to resign themselves to disagreement or criticism despite their sweeping claim.

He let the axe drop and faced me deliberately, 'Now, let me see your face.' He seemed to be looking so hard at me, into me, searching for something, not for him but for me. Finally his stare relaxed and he lifted his gaze out across the lake and pointed, 'There. Have you been up there yet?'

He was pointing to a high ridgeline out beyond and above the redwoods, what looked like a short plateau that sat at the base of where the steep mountains suddenly made their vertical ascent. 'No, no I haven't,' I said squinting into the morning sun.

'Well, put on your shoes because that's where we're going.'

We followed an old Indian trail through the southern woods; the leaves of the oaks and maples shifted pleasantly in the breeze; the canopy dark but not gloomy. We walked mostly in silence. I was absorbing everything that I passed; soaking in a new understanding and appreciation, becoming intimately aware, or perhaps better, *attuned* to the relationship with nature the further we went. I felt a sense of dissolving, a dissolving of that hallucination of separateness so eloquently explained to me last night. I felt the trunks of the trees, the moss draping over boulders, the air that carried a blackbird overhead. The earth beneath my feet seemed to penetrate my soul with each step. It was an extraordinary sensation. *The leaf in the wind.*

My guest only spoke to point out something worth mentioning: a particularly beautiful flower, a lizard in the rushes, that sort of thing. We eventually passed the redwoods and then the forest reduced itself to smaller, thinner conifers. The ground was harder and rockier, and the soil not so soft. We reached the steppe that rose slowly and became the mountain; the rich colours of the forest turned to faded yellows and dusty browns. Now out in the open the sun beat down on us; it was a spring sun so it was gentle but we were sweaty and breathing heavily soon enough. We hiked steadily up the steeping face and across the rocky surface with seemingly no end in sight. I'm not sure if we were following a path or not but we made our way by climbing in long diagonal slants back and forth across the face of the mountain. The peaks were too high above us to see them but I felt I could walk on forever.

After a while I stopped to see how far we had come; the lake glistened like opal, the forest a thick patchwork of unbroken green except for that lovely lime birch on the north side, the cabin invisible. I felt on top of the world despite how much more there was to go; but it wasn't a daunting feeling, rather one of exhilaration and anticipation.

The day wore on, the sun crossing its midpoint and had even begun its way down. It had gotten tougher over the last hour or so; the climb steeper and the rock more unforgiving. My back ached, my thighs were heavy and I had grazed my knees and elbows repeatedly. We climbed in silence; my guest always at my heels, urging me on with his closeness. The joy of the expedition had taken a turn at some point; I couldn't think when. *One step after the other.* Thoughts drifted, blurring into one another. 'How much further do you think?'

'How much further do you want?' He replied.

I took it to mean how much further could I go on still enjoying the climb, still enjoying the test of his company and the challenges he offered. *He must be tired too.* The sun dropped further and became a gorgeous orange and the sky transitioned from light to dark blue over our heads. It had become a battle I thought, a test of wills. And now I was utterly spent, I wanted to stop, to tell him this was far enough, this was as far as I could go.

'Look up, my dear boy,' I heard him say from behind.

I lifted my head; it was the plateau. I had made it. I had conquered something I hadn't even realised I was fighting and it felt amazing. I walked around the small, flattened area that overlooked the valley below; the sun was slipping through the trees and now everything below had that dark blue tint to it. The thought crossed my mind how he knew of this place, almost imperceptible from below but I was filled with too much jubilation, and exhaustion. The plateau was unusually flat; one side dropped at a sheer edge while the other side backed up against the mountain that continued up and up. There was a small alcove with a fire-pit dug out in front of it, and there were old blankets and pieces of brittle firewood, ancient looking, stacked in the recess and covered in inches of dust.

'You sit and relax,' he said, 'I'll get a fire going.'

The stars slowly began to turn on and the sun had dropped out of sight. It was about to get cold but thankfully the fire took quickly. We beat the dust from the blankets and settled in for the night; our backs to the wall, our eyes to the edge of tomorrow. Neither of us spoke for a while; the view too glorious to interrupt. The fire crackled and licked the cool air, and little embers popped and flew off living for just a moment; just an eternity.

'He, who having cast off the world would desire to return again? He would be only there,'[1] my guest said quietly, and no more to me than the flames before us.

I watched him a moment, 'I'm sorry?'

He turned to me, 'And yet, so long as one is alive, life will call.' He smiled hollowly, his face glowing yellow in the firelight, 'Society, that place where men are fractions imagine themselves to be complete, is jealous of those who remain away from it, and will come knocking.'

His mood was strange and sombre; an air of melancholy surrounded him but I had a certain realisation to what he was saying. 'This is not life, is it?' I asked, 'This is only the preparation for it.'

'Yes,' he said slowly, 'and so I've come to tell you that it is time to go back. You have rejected a great deal of many things, many things part and parcel of existing within the modern world; but now it is time to take the treasures you have discovered in the deep and return, otherwise you offer nothing.'

'The modern world you say, with its passing joys and sorrows, banalities and obscenities of life,' I replied whimsically.

'Ah, yes, why even attempt to make plausible or even interesting to men and women consumed with passion the experience of transcendental bliss?[2] I'll tell you why, my dear boy. Because the soul-satisfying vision *is* temporary, and the need is paramount to make it lasting.' He recast one of those long searching stares before continuing, 'The concern is not that people will not listen, it is the necessity that you speak. The people willing and ready will hear you and that is all you can hope for.'

'But why suffer that?'

'You'll suffer only if you make it so. Like you have been. The sorrow of our existence is overcome not through logic or reasoning by our misguided ego but rather the submission of our consciousness to the ineffable, the all, the universe, which understands both the necessity of existence and the joy therein. This is the will to live. And because you are alive, because you do exist, that is the very and only proof you need. *Remember, you are the universe personified.*'

His voice rose and he spoke imploringly. 'So long as you are alive, you always have the chance to be happy. This hope lies within us all. Ultimately, the hope of meaning and purpose, of love and happiness, not just to each other but to all living things, makes the pain of existence bearable. We inherently love life not because we are born used to living but because something in us is used to loving, connecting, creating. This hope and purpose is our consolation as we weave this world and dream a dance of others in which we attempt to define our own true self, never forgetting the limitless paradise from which we sprang.

'You have chosen a hard path, harder than most

dream of treading, and you've done it at the risk of being tragically misunderstood. But I'm sorry to say that is the cost, the cost of being a boon-bringer. What use is possessing knowledge if you fail to become the messenger of it? Remember, he who has not the spirit of this age, has all the misery of it.'[3] He stopped a moment, calming his thoughts before speaking them, 'If the self is the other, and the part is the whole, if each atom contains in itself the universe, then what is done by one individual affects all others; as he raises himself, he so too raises the whole universe.'[4]

A reminiscent thought came to me, 'A rising tide to lift all ships...' I whispered absently.

'Exactly, my dear boy. Do not long for a romantic version of the past that may have never existed, but concern yourself with only what lies before you. The less people apply themselves to this complete, human endeavour, well, the harder it becomes for those already doing it. Whether we like it or not, change comes, and the greater the resistance, the greater the pain.'[5]

We watched the fire crackle away while our rocky precipice slowly spun on its axis. The stars stayed still but we moved and then we could no longer see some of them anymore.

'Will,' he said in that calm, deliberate tone, 'show me your face.'

It was that same request I had heard time and time again. First in my dream, then with Isabelle, the old woman had asked it too. And now him, all asking to see my face.

'Show me,' he continued, 'the face which you had before your mother and father conceived you.'

But here it was, in its complete question, its full form, its absolute riddle. The Japanese call it a *koan*; a paradox to be meditated upon and used to abandon our dependence on reason and force one into gaining sudden intuitive enlightenment. How could I show him my face before I became myself? I looked searchingly into the fire, groping for some kind of meaning, some trick to unravel the key. But I had been here so long I had almost forgotten what I had even looked like; perhaps I had forgotten. More embers popped and fizzled and the larger pieces of wood had become white and charred underneath. With enough time the primordial flame would dissolve the wood back to a more elemental form and return it to the universe. I turned and I looked into his fiery reflecting eyes and said, 'I'm showing it to you, aren't I? I've always been showing it to you.'

'Yes,' he said smiling, putting a hand on my shoulder, 'you have.'

He looked back out over the edge, out to the wonderful wilderness and the infinite cosmos after that. 'We are all visitors to this time and place. We are just passing through. Our purpose here is to observe, to learn, to grow, to love... and then we return home.[6] All things are in process, rising and returning. Plants come to blossom, but only to return to the root. Returning to the root is like seeking tranquillity. Seeking tranquillity is like moving toward destiny. To move toward destiny is like eternity. To know eternity is enlightenment, and not to recognise eternity brings disorder and suffering. Knowing eternity makes one comprehensive; comprehension makes one broadminded; breadth of vision brings nobility; nobility is like heaven.'[7]

We sat in long silence once again. My mind absorbing yet another layer of understanding; another non-conceptual perspective of reality taking root in my awareness, my consciousness. For once it wasn't all too much to handle, to take in; aspects of me, a deeper self, had been opened and had made room for this new knowledge, this I now knew. All that sorrow, grief, and anger I once felt was perhaps a measure of my humanity or spiritual maturity.[8] And before coming here, into this quiet wilderness, I felt that my heart and soul was thoroughly torn open, but now those wounds were healed, healed by knowledge and understanding. And nature; the mother of us all.

'How long have I been there, in that cabin?'

'Who am I to say? But it has not been days but months; and if not months then years in the making, my dear boy.'

'Why does it take so long?'

'Because the poetry of our spiritual past has been killed; science and history and now even religion have belittled its purpose and so there is no life left in it. Of course mythology under such a microscope becomes absurd, but was it ever meant to stand up to empiricism or fact? Remember, forms and concepts are there to guide the mind towards openness and beyond, to make possible and then to facilitate the jump into that very abyss we all have inside us. And so all gods and religions are but a convenient and eloquent means, descriptions themselves from our very own grasping for names and terms, but used nonetheless to move and awaken the mind, to call it past itself in the hopes of reconnecting it with the ineffable.[9] The journey of transcendental bliss is not grasped easily, now more so than ever, only the soul who has dared to plunge into the abyss of the unknown to touch it can begin his return voyage, and this takes courage, courage few have that are willing to die and be reborn again within the same lifetime.'

He turned to me, 'This is your task at hand; you've become aware of what lies beyond and now you must return and attempt to knit together the two worlds.'[10]

I knew this before he said it. I realised it was why I had come here in the first place; this cabin in the wilderness, the gnawing in my stomach, his arrival, his knocking... this man with the familiar face.

'It is time to go back and see the sun rise for the first time, my dear boy, for it is no longer the evening land[11] you once understood it to be.'

'I know. I am ready.'

He smiled warmly, crinkling the corners of his eyes, 'Good.'

'What will you do?' I asked after a moment.

'Me? I don't know. Perhaps I'll stay here a while.'

'Well, will you look after it for me? I may wish to come back one day.'

'Oh, it'll be like you never left.'

We watched more stars shift across the sky and the

fire burn low atop a bed of white ash. An owl gave a fateful hoot somewhere far above us.

'Well, old friend, the hour has grown late and I am weary,' he yawned, 'and sleep beckons for us both.'

We lay down next to the dying fire; the rocky floor not so uncomfortable beneath our blankets. Closing my eyes I thought of another life, another person I used to know, and wondered how well we'll get along. A new energy flowed within me; an energy that cannot be broken nor time decay. I went to sleep smiling. Now I am nimble, now I fly, now I see myself under myself, now a god dances within me.[12]

PART IV

TWENTY
A WAY TO GO

THE CURTAINS STRUGGLED to hold off the morning light as I blinked my eyes open to the blinding grey that filled my apartment. I sat up on my elbows and vaguely observed the cracked corners of the wall, the peeling paint, the upturned book I must have been reading last night – all those irrelevant things that only leap out at you in those first few moments of nonsensical wakefulness. I got up stiffly and walked over to the drapes that covered the wide bay window and pulled them apart. The diffused yellow light burst in and I had to close my eyes; I could feel the warmth of the sunshine on my face as I slowly unfurrowed my brow. I looked out over the city, bright and yet hazy, the white spring air shining on everything. It felt good to be home.

I lit the stove, got some coffee going, and showered. As the water ran over me, visions flashed of another time and place, a cabin in the woods, gone but not forgotten. I rubbed the mirror down and checked who I saw; a face so familiar and yet one that was living just one of his thousand lives. I laughed and the coffee pot whistled. I threw on some clothes and poured myself a mug of black before going up to the rooftop.

There was a cool breeze that prickled my skin but the sun was becoming steadily warmer. I clutched at the coffee to heat my hands and inhaled its pleasant brew. I sat and watched schooners and yachts move slowly about the bay, now glistening, and cars begin to fill the uptown. I started to drink my coffee and the sun rose a little higher; tram dings' soon echoed and people's voices could be heard on the street below. *What a ride*, I thought gladly.

I wondered how so little could change and yet I could feel so differently about the plight of mankind. And I realised it was all perspective and understanding; and understanding of oneself most of all. And the catch was, we cannot simply be told the answer to our woes. And that's not to say the answers aren't there because they are, repeated time and again throughout history. But the fact remains you cannot be told today how you should behave and think and feel tomorrow; that realisation is gradual, developed and pursued over time, and it must come from within you, after some effort, from discovering your true self; what you are, who you are, why you are. And until these questions are answered by you to at least some critical degree, simply being told the answer won't help, nor will following old methods of living bring fulfilment to your own. That direction has been exhausted for some time and to follow it further is to welcome the suffering it carries with it.

I swirled the coffee around and thought of that night up here with Harvey, the last real conversation we'd had. I felt then nothing could save me from the journey I was on; that dark night spent wandering in the wilderness of which no one could spare me, of which no one could save me. Well, it came and what I lost cannot be called a loss for I am greater now than I was before. But, having crossed that bridge to the other side and surviving the deep loneliness of utter abandonment, perhaps it is easier for me to say so.

And, as well and good as it is for me to speak so astutely, the truth of it is, until you discover it for yourself, you'll never discover yourself. And despite the similarities of me sitting across from you, and the undeniable self-contradictory image being presented, there is a great chasm, an abyss even, seen and felt, traversed and conquered, that lies between us, he who is self-aware and he who is common. We both see mountains as mountains, trees as trees, and rivers as rivers, but there is a perception of it all that cannot be ignored nor understood until at once the common man sees the unreality of his reality. So, until then, one might argue that he is not really living, he is merely pretending. He is at best that veneer above the muckheap. He is living other peoples' ideas and beliefs, he is living other peoples' values and expectations, he is living inside a culture that doesn't belong to him. And what attests to this is that the vast majority of people have so little to show for themselves. This unexamined life is one that goes without a purpose of its own, without cultivating that of which destiny it should follow. The unexamined life is what leads one astray and allows one to be trodden on, no matter how gently, to become scribblers of nothing.

It would be flagrant of me to say that there is not hope in the common man (the bourgeois, the West, modern society), for it does have, but it is by large an empty hope, a false hope simply and because we still lack the necessary virtues to transcend its hollow ideals for sincere action. For sadly, what can a thinking man truly hope for humanity given our past? Very little, if he is being honest. And if I may paint one last crude picture then let it be this: deny me that the following man is not found in great number, he who finds no relevant role in society, who is unneeded by his country, who lives a public, showy life of egotistical self-absorption, engages in futile or purposeless affairs and yet speaks grandly, romantically, or shamelessly about that which he knows little of, protecting his vulnerability and self-despair with meaningless gestures of importance; he may be educated, eloquent and yet utterly superficial, his high ideals have never been tested by reality. He has no moment of truth, no great war to fight, no revolution on his street. His love for himself is greater than anything he sees before him and so sees nothing greater than himself.[1] Am I mistaken? Is the tragedy of being mediocre not evoking an anxiety in us to snatch at that that will save us despite how empty the living? If I am wrong than my life is dust but if there is some truth in it then this is our great challenge; to realise it, realise the emptiness at the core of our modern existence and the disarray of our moral convictions, to realign our motivation and purpose in life to live in better harmony with the rest of life. We must go out and meet it, that which calls for us in our darkest moments, in our silence, and be willing enough, and bold enough to take that leap and discover new lands with new sets values which may only have meaning simply because we have willed them to. And yet never forgetting that life and reality are not things you can keep for yourself unless you accord them to all others.

The paramount question is: what prevents us? The simple misunderstanding of ourselves within the greater universal context. It is not that we come into this world; we come out of it, like leaves from a tree. Each individual is an expression of the whole realm of nature.[2] And we will continue to fall into endless self-regression until we fully realise that there is something that is both proceeding and beyond our human existence; that very energy which permeates the whole universe. This is us and this is our true reality; call it what you will. This is what lies before us; man embracing the truths of our greater cosmic reality from which we have sprung forth, and ultimately, transcending them, so as for a brief moment no longer seeing mountains as mountains and realising that we are the outcome of the fundamental fabric of existence from which we manifest ourselves and construct our subjective reality, and that we are bound by it more so than any religion, any history, or any ideology that contradicts the notion that we are anything but energy condensed to a slow vibration[3] that creates the illusion of matter, form, and object... life as *we* know it.

I finished my coffee and basked in the spring sun; reflecting how each day comes bearing with it the opportunity for something new to happen, to take hold. There was no more drudgery, no more despair; I had had my fill and it offered no salvation. A period I cannot look back on with regret for we are not what merely happens to us; we are what we have chosen to become and those choices are made by us alone.

I left the rooftop with its schooners and yachts and haloed buildings, and came back into my apartment. The open bay window showed that a thin layer of dust had settled on all the surfaces as this life went undisturbed for however long. I walked around the apartment with an almost forgotten memory of it all; I fingered through stacks of books, stared reminiscently at prints on the walls, held a carving or a statue and smiled at the long lost emotions of the adventures that went with it. I picked up the stack of unopened mail; mostly bank statements telling me how much I didn't have, reminders for life insurance, subscriptions to periodicals that had expired, and so on. But at the bottom was a large manila envelope addressed in my own handwriting though I couldn't remember ever sending myself anything. I turned it over to read the return address but all that was written was, 'life in the woods.'[4] I opened it and slid out some typed papers. I smiled to myself and went over to the bay window, delicately framing the world beyond.

Perhaps I am not the latecomer, but the newcomer. To suffer that this world has no intrinsic meaning is a view wasted on what lies beautiful before him. Bazarov you old fool; you were utterly right and yet your answers fed your soul none and you starved.[5] There is a glorious world out there and perhaps not for the first time are we beginning to realise that it goes beyond our immediate passions and sensations, beyond the groping hand of the egotistical and self-serving. And isn't this where Jake and Brett and Robert let their hearts go astray?[6] For anyone who grabs a sliver of beauty and insists that it is the whole becomes a fanatic, workaholic, cynic, fundamentalist, drug addict, or what have you. Unaware that to live so is to break the tension and tear the fabric of living in a universe rich in allurement and wonder is to move toward the needless destruction of pursuing a partial vision.[7]

No, for how dare you die before you have truly lived. And what is true living? Have I not already tried to point you in that direction? We are there, all of us, the part in the whole, the leaf in the wind, on the precipice of our next great overcoming. All that is needed, willingly or unwillingly, is to leap into that deep abyss, and realise the hags and dragons of our nightmares are in fact the gods and goddesses of a world we already know,[8] a forgotten dimension of who we are.

We have come a long way, but still not long enough. We are not the great end to which humanity repeatedly claims itself complete. There remains that tightrope, that bridge too few of us risk crossing despite the necessity to do so. Although we may no longer be breeding an apathetic creature, we nurture it still and in doing so tell it to grow with no great passion or commitment, unable to dream, who merely earns his living and keeps warm at the cost of casting his fellow man out into the cold.

Dare I suggest, and despite its somewhat resurgence, that we have unconsciously thrown off our threadbare nihilistic cloak; he who would rather lapse into silence than reveal the extent of his hopeful dreams to an uncomprehending world, now only to wander purposelessly in at last a world capable of comprehending him but who is kept dreamless. We are still largely avoiding and denying our own emptiness; and despite all we know and all we can know, we remain clueless to the jewel of our existence. We still have a way to go... and until then, so dark shall remain the con of man.

END NOTES

Foreword:
1. Gogol, *Dead Souls*, pp. xx
2. de Botton, *How Proust Can Change Your Life*, pp. 73

Part I

Chapter One: A Tear Welled
1. Ryokan, *Dewdrops On A Lotus Leaf*, pp. xx

Chapter Two: Den of the Bellyachers

Chapter Three: Lost For Words
Hermann Hesse's depiction of the human psyche as a wolf (of the steppe) is used here as an archetype that initially represents the character Will; hence the repeated similarities in description and context early on. However, this 'archetype' is much sooner overcome, and acts as a steppingstone for the extended theme of this story.
1. Hesse, *Steppenwolf*, pp. 39
2. Much of this passage is a modernised version, felt originally by Will, as what Hesse described his character Harry Haller as being torn by (Hesse, *Steppenwolf*, pp. 39).
3. *Immortal* is used here and throughout to refer to any individual who has had a profound and lasting effect on humanity.
4. Campbell, *The Hero With A Thousand Faces*, pp. 51

5. Hesse, *Steppenwolf*, pp. 64
6. Hesse, *Steppenwolf*, pp. 64
7. Hesse, *Steppenwolf*, pp. 65
8. Hesse, *Steppenwolf*, pp. 65
9. Hesse, Steppenwolf, pp. 66
10. *Mathew 10:39*, KJV
11. Hesse, *Steppenwolf*, pp. 73

Chapter Four: In Her Heart of Hearts

Chapter Five: That'll Be All, Bill
1. Albert Einstein

Chapter Six: This is Nothing New
1. Essentially an old independent or repertory theatre he inherited from his grandfather.
2. Charles 'Chuck' Palahniuk, author of *Fight Club*.
3. *Ubermensch* (in German) or *superman, overman, higher person, higher being*, etc. is a concept of philosopher Friedrich Nietzsche who posited the *ubermensch* as a goal for humanity with which we would create our own values and reasons for living in a world where all gods were dead.
4. de Botton, *How Proust Can Change Your Life*, pp. 75

Chapter Seven: A Rope Over an Abyss
1. This passage reflects the same anticipatory psychological and emotional uprooting transformation that most people will experience at various periods in their life; it is heavily influenced by Jungian *Individual Psychology*, and

is adapted from, Hesse, *Steppenwolf*, pp. 81, despite it being universally experienced.

2. *Steppenwolf*, pp. 82

3. Alan Watts, *Become What You Are*, pp. 1

4. In the story *Steppenwolf*, Harry receives a pamphlet titled *Treatise on the Steppenwolf*; this passage is a loose summary.

5. This is the conclusion Hesse's character Harry came to at the end of *Steppenwolf*.

6. Jung, *Four Archetypes*, pp. 108

7. Nietzsche, *Thus Spoke Zarathustra*, pp. 43-44

8. *Thus Spoke Zarathustra*, pp. 39

9. *Thus Spoke Zarathustra*, pp. 41

1. Alvin Toffler, *Rethinking The Future*, pp. xx

2. Watts, *The Book: on the taboo of knowing who you are*, pp. 45

1. Watts, *The Book: on the taboo of knowing who you are*, pp. 137

2. This paraphrase, and the following passage and additional explanation of the participation mystique is adapted from, Jung, *Four Archetypes*, pp. 60-61

3. See note 1

4. See note 1

5. *Philemon 1:1-20*, KJ
6. This description that God would impart infinite wisdom on illiterate goat herders is paraphrased from a speech by Christopher Hitchens.
7. *1 Corinthians 14:34-35*, KJV
8. Selections from *Nietzsche's notebooks of the early 1870s*, pp. 3
9. Watts, *Become What You Are*, pp. 31-32
10. The King James Version was completed by eight members of the Church of England only a few hundred years ago. They used no original texts to translate from because there are none. The oldest manuscripts ever found were written down hundreds of years after the last apostle died, and there are over eight-thousand of these manuscripts with hundreds of known and unknown authors, and with no two alike. The King James translators edited already translated versions of unoriginal manuscripts to create a tailored version of the bible the Parliament and the King of England would approve.
11. Watts, *Become What You Are*, pp. 83
12. Watts, *Become What You Are*, pp. 102
13. Watts, *This Is It*, pp. 89
14. See note 11
15. Watts, *The Book: on the taboo of knowing who you are*, pp. 80
16. This passage is paraphrased from Joseph Campbell's, *The Hero With A Thousand Faces*, pp. 104
17. Nietzsche, *Thus Spoke Zarathustra*, pp. xx

18. Campbell, *The Hero With A Thousand Faces*, pp. 387

19. Campbell, *The Hero With A Thousand Faces*, pp. 388

20. Shared sentiments from Watts, *This Is It*, pp. 134-135

21. See note 20

22. *Amor fati*: Latin phrase loosely translating to 'love of one's fate,' reflecting one's attitude in which everything that happens, including suffering and loss, is seen as good or necessary.

23. Nietzsche was actually beyond nihilism; his philosophies explained extensively how one was to overcome it.

24. Nietzsche, section 276 of, *The Gay Sciences*

25. Watts, *The Book: on the taboo of knowing who you are*, pp. 142

Part II

Chapter Twelve: Sad and Glimmering

Chapter Thirteen: Let Me Take You Somewhere

1. French: literally, 'five to seven,' colloquial for an evening tryst.

2. French: formal greeting, 'I am delighted to get acquainted with you.'

3. This list is taken, as an ode – meaning that nothing has since changed, from Watts, *The Book: on the taboo of knowing who you are*, pp. 114

4. Watts, *The Book: on the taboo of knowing who you are*, pp. 112

5. Hesse, *Steppenwolf*, pp. 73-76

Chapter Fourteen: Homesickness
This story is adapted from a Native American Indian folktale, *Legends and Lore of Texas Wildflowers*, by Elizabeth Silverthorne, Texas A&M University Press, 2002

1. This passage mirrors Hermione's conversation with Harry in much the same way Isabelle reveals her knowledge of Will, *Steppenwolf*, pp. 175
2. 'Most men will not swim before they are able to,' said by Novalis and quoted in *Steppenwolf*, pp. 21. Isabelle then applies this explanation to Will's over-thinking torment.
3. Hesse, *Steppenwolf*, pp. 204
4. Hesse, *Steppenwolf*, pp. 204
5. Hermione to Harry, *Steppenwolf*, pp. 180
6. Turgenev, *First Love & Other Stories*, pp.177
7. French: 'to have sweet dreams.'

Chapter Fifteen: All That I Am

1. This dream is a combination of two Buddhist myths. The person, presumably Will, riding the blue lion is Mañjuśrī, a bodhisattva associated with transcendent wisdom. The demon is Yamāntaka, a wrathful manifestation of Mañjuśrī but also a Buddha; it is thought that when one adopts the practice of Yamāntaka (who is often depicted as dancing and crushing the bodies of fellow gods) they are practicing the termination of death; or, that which is beyond identity, form, worship, following, etc., they are meditating on

stopping the cycle of rebirth, samsara, and going beyond it, to enlightenment. The second myth is that of *Prince Five-Weapons*, who, after exhausting himself in battle against an ogre is eventually caught, however, he has contained within him the weapon of knowledge that defeats his enemy (Campbell, *The Hero With A Thousand Faces*, pp. 85-89).

Chapter Sixteen: For That You Must Perish

1. Hesse, *Steppenwolf*, pp. 22
2. Swimme, *The Universe Is A Green Dragon*, pp. 35
3. Hesse, *Steppenwolf*, pp. 28
4. *Symplegades*: in Greek mythology were a pair of rocks that clashed together, and were eventually defeated by Jason and the Argonauts, after which the rocks stopped moving permanently.
5. This notion of being caught between two ages belongs to Oswald Spengler's somewhat controversial social criticism, *The Decline Of The West*, (1926)
6. This phrase is adapted from Benjamin Franklin who said, 'Justice will not be served until those who are unaffected are as outraged as those who are.'
7. See note 5: this idea is further extrapolated here through the old woman's demonstration with the budding and dying daisy flowers.
8. Jung, *Four Archetypes*, pp. 55
9. Talbot, *The Holographic Universe*, pp. 288

10. The hallucinogenic plant described here is *atropa belladona*, however, this flower and fruit delivers a most unpleasant and often terrifying experience, and it has been only employed here because it is visually prettier to illustrate. The actual medicinal plant that sends Will on the next stage of his journey is *Ayahuasca*, which he did in fact consume in Peru, South America.
11. Talbot, *The Holographic Universe*, pp. 302
12. Adapted from Campbell, *The Hero With A Thousand Faces*, pp. 261
13. Bach, *Illusions*, pp. 126
14. Nietzsche, *Thus Spoke Zarathustra*, pp. 69

Part III

Chapter Seventeen: Forest for the Trees
1. *Brothers Karamazov*, Dostoyevsky; *Fathers and Sons*, Turgenev; *Dead Souls*, Gogol; *The Steppe and Other Short Stories*, Chekhov; *Sketches From A Sportsman's Notebook*, Turgenev
2. Hemingway, Faulkner, Fitzgerald, Steinbeck, Salinger, Vonnegut

Chapter Eighteen: Snow Falling on the Windowsill
The stunning clarity with which Alan Watts explains, untangles, and recasts Eastern and Western religions, philosophies, and ideologies, and places them in a greater, universal context is paramount, in the author's opinion, to developing a broader understanding of humanity, its religious history, and its intention on humanity both culturally and spiritually. As Will enters

the final stage of his cathartic journey, several of Watt's publications are drawn upon to express and describe Will's situation, and to offer a context and resolution to his situation.

1. Watts, *The Nature Of Consciousness*, pp. xx
2. Adapted sentiments from, Watts, *Become What You Are*, pp. 74
3. Watts, *Become What You Are*, pp. 4-5
4. Campbell, *The Hero With A Thousand Faces*, pp. 236
5. Watts, *Become What You Are*, pp. 13
6. Watts, *Become What You Are*, pp. 34
7. Watts, *Become What You Are*, pp. 121-122
8. Watts, *This Is It*, pp. 23
9. Carl Sagan, 'The nitrogen in our DNA, the calcium in our teeth, the iron in our blood, the carbon in our apple pies were made in the interiors of collapsing stars. We are made of starstuff.'
10. Adapted sentiments from, Swimme, *The Universe Is A Green Dragon*, pp. 58-59
11. Watts, *The Book: on the taboo of knowing who you are*, pp. 92
12. Watts, *The Book: on the taboo of knowing who you are*, pp. 130-131
13. Watts, *Become What You Are*, pp. 126
14. Watts, *The Book: on the taboo of knowing who you are*, pp. 124-125
15. Watts, *The Book: on the taboo of knowing who you are*, pp. 121
16. This parable of a Buddhist monk is fictional; it was written to house the sentiment of the story, a

view expressed by Watts, *Become What You Are*, pp. 131

17. Further extrapolation of note 16

18. Watts, *The Book: on the taboo of knowing who you are*, pp. 53

19. Talbot, *The Holographic Universe*, pp. 285

20. Jung, *Four Archetypes*, pp. 54

21. Swimme, *The Universe Is A Green Dragon*, pp. 31

22. Isaac Asimov, 'The saddest aspect of life right now is that science gathers knowledge faster than society gathers wisdom.'

23. Talbot, *The Holographic Universe*, pp. 265

24. Talbot, *The Holographic Universe*, pp. 160

25. Quote by Leo Tolstoy

Chapter Nineteen: Nobility is Like Heaven

1. Campbell, *The Hero With A Thousand Faces*, pp. 207, quoting *Jaimuniya Upanishad Brahmana*

2. Campbell, *The Hero With A Thousand Faces*, pp. 218

3. Quote by Voltaire

4. Watts, *Become What You Are*, pp. 103

5. Watts, *Become What You Are*, pp. 60

6. Australian Aboriginal Proverb

7. Campbell, *The Hero With A Thousand Faces*, pp. 189

8. Joanna Macy, *World As Lover, World As Self*, pp. 152

9. Loosely paraphrased from, Campbell, *The Hero With A Thousand Faces*, pp. 258

10. Adapted from, Campbell, *The Hero With A Thousand Faces*, pp. 228

11. Spengler explained that the title of his book, *The Decline Of The West* (German: *Der Untergang Des Abendlandes*), was not meant to imply some sort of catastrophe that would bring the downfall of the West; *Sonnenuntergang* is German for sunset, and so his referral to the West was more accurately that it would see its twilight, its evening, its final 'going under.'

12. See note 14, Chapter Sixteen: For That You Must Perish

Part IV

Chapter Twenty: A Way to Go

1. The above description portrays the qualities of Turgenev's superfluous man, *Rudin*.

2. Watts, *The Book: On the taboo of knowing who you are*, pp. 9

3. Reference to Bill Hicks, 'Today a young man on acid realized that all matter is merely energy condensed to a slow vibration, that we are all one consciousness experiencing itself subjectively, there is no such thing as death, life is only a dream, and we are the imagination of ourselves.'

4. Henry David Thoreau's, *Walden*, was a work of personal declaration of independence, social experiment, voyage of spiritual discovery, satire, and manual for self-reliance in which he documents the experiences he had over the two

years, two months, and two days he spent in a cabin he built amidst woodland near Concord, Massachusetts. It was first published as, *Walden, or Life in the Woods*.

5. Bazarov of *Fathers and Sons*, Turgenev's quintessential nihilist of nineteenth-century Russia, wanted to break the bonds of social convention, or be broken himself; he rejected the illusions of romance and generational reconciliation, instead embracing the only road he saw fit for a young man of his time: one of empiricism, materialism, and a socially engaged form of nihilism. However, all he gets out of life is the deathbed kiss of the woman he unwillingly loves.

6. Jake, Brett, and Robert: the main protagonists of Hemingway's *Fiesta*, are part of the 'lost generation' of post-WWI America/England; a world devoid of strong social beliefs, defined ultimately by meaningless personal conduct who fill their lives with sexual excess, drunken forgetfulness, and selfish satisfactions.

7. Swimme, *The Universe Is A Green Dragon*, pp. 79-80

8. Campbell, The Hero With A Thousand Faces, pp. 217

BIBLIOGRAPHY

In the interest of honouring the works that inspired the character and this story, I am listing not only the texts that have been paraphrased or referenced, but also those that have had a profound effect on me and on the retelling of this story.

Turgenev, I., *Fathers and Sons*, Penguin Classics, England, 2009 (first published 1862).

Turgenev, I., *Sketches from a Huntsman's Album*, Penguin Classics, England, 1990 (first published 1852).

Hemingway, E., *Fiesta: The sun also rises*, Vintage Books, London, 2000 (first published 1926).

Swimme, B., *The Universe Is A Green Dragon*, Bear & Company, Vermont, 1984.

Watts, A., *Become What You Are*, Shambhala Publications, Massachusetts, 1995.

Watts, A., *This Is It*, Vintage Books, New York, 1973.

Watts, A., *The Book: On the taboo of knowing who you are*, Souvenir Press, London, 2009 (first published 1966).

Nietzsche, F., *Thus Spoke Zarathustra*, Penguin Classics, England, 2003 (first published 1883).

Hesse, H, *Steppenwolf*, Penguin Books, Australia, 2009 (first published 1927).

Bach, R., *Illusions: The adventures of a reluctant messiah*, Dell Publishing, New York, 1977.

Campbell, J., *The Hero With A Thousand Faces*, Fontana Press, London, 1993 (first published 1949).

Talbot, M., *The Holographic Universe*, Harper Collins, London, 1996.

Jung, C. G., *Four Archetypes*, Princeton University Press, New Jersey, 2010 (first published 1970).

9 780099 433800 6